Maps, Mockingbirds, and Misdeeds

Riley Creek Cozy Mystery Series, Volume 3

Mary Lucal

Published by Mary Lucal, 2023.

MAPS, MOCKINGBIRDS, AND MISDEEDS

First edition. June 1, 2023.

Written by Mary Lucal.

From the Diary of Charlton Riley, held in the Special Collections Room at the Riley Creek Public Library

BARRINGTON, ENGLAND, January 1890

It is time for me to take my leave, regardless of Mother's wish for me to wait another few months. It's hard to express things so honestly—I would never wish to add to her burden after Father's passing, but find I must. My brother Cyril runs our estate with a steady hand, having prepared well at Father's knee, but I ask here in these pages: what is left for me? Really, society is unkind in its expectations. We second, third and fourth sons cannot inherit from our fathers, yet we are expected somehow to make our way and profit without dirtying our hands too thoroughly in the process.

Cyril has kindly offered to keep me on here with a reasonable allowance, but what life is that? And what young woman would want to join such a household, watched over as we would be by Mother and Cyril? No, I am going to Liverpool, and from there I shall sail over the Atlantic to Boston.

Several aid societies in London have partnered with their like-minded brethren in Boston to create what they call "transplant communities" for disenfranchised people and their families. There is such a community planned at the foot of the mountains in the southern state of Tennessee, and I have decided that this is my destination. I am told that land is plentiful, rivers and creeks flow throughout, and young men of intelligence and fortitude will prosper there. I was a strong pupil at school and am eager to learn those industrial arts which so far I have only observed.

I suppose there, I will encounter other second sons like me, and together we will start a new community. Think of it! A chance to begin anew, without the trappings of class, society, and expectation. We shall be like Adam, but able to right our fathers' mistakes! Unlike Cyril, I will have the pride of knowing that my new life was entirely built by my own two hands.

I confess I am nervous tonight as I prepare to tell Mother and Cyril of my plans. But I shall convince them that my destiny lies not here in Britain, but rather in the United States of America.

Chapter One

"This isn't the time to take a *call*!" hollered PJ. She stood, muscled arms crossed, watching two lanes of bowling action. Uncrossing her arms, she then used one manicured index finger to point at the rhinestone-studded Apple watch on her other wrist.

"We only have the lanes till seven!" Then she was distracted by Carl and Joanne, who had paused their practice throws to laugh at a shared joke. As PJ turned to bring the full weight of her tan velour gym-suited figure to bear on her teammates, Martha snatched the opportunity to move away to take the incoming call. As she answered, she walked toward the snack bar where she could hear herself over the sound of pins crashing.

"Hey, Ana, how are you? It's great to hear from you," Martha said, trying to sound breezy. As she listened to the voice coming down the line, she thought how convenient it was to be able to receive calls now that the cell reception in Riley Creek had improved. After another thirty seconds, she found herself missing the days when she sometimes wouldn't hear news—good or bad—for days.

"It's totally fine," Martha said. "I get it. And I *know* you're doing everything you can." She paused and listened again. "Yes, absolutely, Ana. Everything here is fine, business is steady, so just focus on things there. Right. Yes. Good to talk to you too. Take care."

Ending the call, Martha reflected that things were definitely *not* fine and business at the shop was *far* from steady. Perhaps the contract to supply beans for the bird research center her friend Ana Moreno was heading would come through, but it wouldn't pay the pile of bills she had waiting for her at home.

PJ's voice rang through her thoughts. "Our shirts may read 'Bowling is for the Birds,' but we've got a title to defend, people."

"Technically, we did not win the title. We came in third," said Carl evenly, a hint of his native German coming through. Carl was a stickler for detail, which Martha thought must be a positive quality for a baker; the baked goods he, his wife Cat and son Lew turned out at An Early Riser were certainly as close to perfection as Martha could imagine. But she wasn't sure PJ appreciated Carl's exactitude right at this moment.

"Look, it was the first time our Birds 'n' Beans team ever placed in any bowling event, and now we've at *least* got a reputation to defend," PJ insisted. "Put your arms into it, people!" She held up her own massive arm and flexed her bicep, keeping her fist open to accommodate her French-tipped nails.

When PJ walked over to give Allison a few pointers, Joanne sidled up to Martha, who'd returned to the Formica table at the head of one of the lanes.

"*Mon dieu*. You'd think we'd placed in the U.S. Olympic Trials and not the East Tennessee Bowling Buddies' Bonanza." She adjusted the flowing black scarf that held her hair back. A retired French teacher and IT aficionado, Joanne had put together a striking outfit for today's practice. From the waist up, she was, as they all were, outfitted in a long-sleeved black t-shirt that read, as PJ had pointed out, "Bowling is for the Birds" on the back in Comic Sans typeface, with "Birds" written down one sleeve and "Beans" up the other. On the chest pocket of each was the Birds 'n' Beans shop logo. From the waist down, though, she sported black spandex and black legwarmers. The whole ensemble ended with the red, white and blue bowling shoes the team rented here at Splitsville Bowlo-rama.

"She's just a proud mama, that's all," Martha said, privately agreeing with Joanne, but refusing to criticize PJ. PJ had been one of her aunt's dearest friends since Lorna had started Birds 'n' Beans, her birding retail and coffee shop. Now that Lorna was deceased and Martha had left Boston to become the shop's owner, she'd found to her happy surprise that PJ had provided her with the same steadfast loyalty. So Martha pinched her lips shut and didn't let on to Joanne that PJ polished the team's third place trophy (which held a place of honor on the wall at Birds 'n' Beans) nearly every day.

Joanne looked skyward, let out a breath, and returned to her lane. Martha got up and blew on her fingertips in preparation for a practice shot, letting Allison take her place in the plastic swivel chair. Short and stout as she was, only the tips of Allison's bowling shoes touched the floor's blonde wood. Running a hand over her spiky dark-red hair, she read the scores on the TV monitor affixed to the ceiling for few moments, then asked Martha what was wrong.

"How do you know anything's wrong?" Martha said innocently. She hadn't planned on sharing the details of Ana's call until she'd had more time to process the news.

"I'm a police officer, remember? I can read people like a book." Then Allison smiled. "I also knew you'd been waiting to hear from Ana, heard you say 'Hey, Ana, how are you?' and saw the worried look on your face when you hung up your phone."

Martha had once again let her Boston side run away with her, automatically avoiding letting anyone in on her business. But Allison was now one of her best friends and Martha knew that meant she could be trusted with the truth.

Friends that find dead bodies together stay together, right?

"Yeah, you're right, the news wasn't good. Ana said the permits to allow construction to begin on the research center still haven't arrived, so they're pushing everything back a few more months." A tragedy involving Ana's father had caused a chance meeting between the two women, and Ana had offered Martha a contract to roast beans for what was to be a state-of-the-art bird conservancy and research center. "Looks like it'll be a few more months' worth of my 401k keeping us afloat," Martha said, blowing out her cheeks.

"But what about the online business?" Allison asked. "Isn't that going to give you a boost?"

"Now that we have a solid internet signal, it'll definitely help, but everything I've read says it takes a while to solidify your *online presence*." These last two words, Martha surrounded with air quotes, using two fingers on each hand. "And I've got bills to pay *right now*." Air quotes again.

"Well, surely the nature writers' retreat will help things," Allison said encouragingly.

This woman could find a silver lining inside Dracula's coffin, Martha thought.

"I sure am hopeful. Speaking of which, I've got to wrap things up here so I can get home and put my head together before tomorrow's Retailers' Collective meeting. We've got to finalize all of our plans for the retreat."

Allison hopped from her chair and the two tossed the last twenty or so balls of the evening. Once PJ was satisfied they'd gotten a good solid practice in, she dismissed the players on her team, but only after they promised to do wrist exercises between now and the next practice.

"Grip strength, people. It's all about grip strength," she said.

Whatever that may be, Martha thought. *I come to Splitsville to gossip and drink craft beer.*

Allison and Martha had ridden to practice together. As Martha drove the short route back to Riley Creek, Allison asked her how she liked being the current president of the R-C, as some in the village had taken to calling the Retailers' Collective.

"Well, since the group itself has only existed since the start of the New Year, I can't help but still feel a little bit like I was heaved onto the members as their leader," Martha replied. This was true—Octavius Bennett, the owner of Toad in a Hole bookshop, PJ, and Frank Elder, owner of the hardware store, had spoken passionately at the group's first meeting about Martha's leadership qualities, leaving little air in the room for any other nomination. Nonetheless, a vote had taken place, during which Martha had waited outside the multipurpose room at the library. PJ had later told her that the *confidential vote* (PJ had winked at this term) had indicated overwhelming support for Martha. She also admitted, after being pressed, that there were a handful of abstentions from some area merchants.

Martha had accepted the nomination, but still obsessed over the abstentions. And now, she found herself saddled with debt *and* leading the R-C.

As if I didn't doubt my decision-making abilities when I took on the shop, now I can take my imposter syndrome to a whole new level!

She dropped Allison off at her house a few blocks from the square, then drove the short distance to her own cottage. Pulling into the driveway in the dark, she felt immediate relief when the security lights mounted on the corner of the house flipped on. The lights were courtesy of her neighbor Jimmy Ritzenwaller, following her latest run-in with a psycho murderess from hell.

This confronting murderers thing is getting to be a habit, thought Martha. *I guess I just attract the wrong kind of person.* Then she thought of the Ritzenwallers, PJ, Allison and all the other wonderful friends she had in Riley Creek, and realized nothing could be further from the truth. Psychopaths, she guessed, were just an occupational hazard of her newfound ability to solve a mystery.

Me, an amateur sleuth, she thought with a grin as she got out of her car. *Who knew*?

Martha bounded up the porch stairs and let herself in to a chorus of barking. Her miniature schnauzer Penny was not impressed and there was a sharpness to the bark that Martha recognized.

"Look, I'm sorry I couldn't take you bowling, but there are rules about such things." The terrier glared at her from under her salt-and-pepper brows. "Yes, *silly and stupid* rules. I totally agree." Penny kept up her racket, undaunted. "OK, OK, simma down now, lady," Martha said, using her best Boston accent and giving Penny a good rub on the head and ears. "You go outside while I find the treat your friend Allison sent you." She opened the French doors on the back of the cottage and Penny headed out to check out the evening's closing news.

By the time Penny had completed a tour of the yard, Martha had rummaged in her backpack, found the homemade peanut butter dog treat from Allison and placed it in the white "Penny's Bowl" near the back door. Penny snatched it up and darted straight to her lambswool bed, where she munched noisily.

"I aim to serve," Martha said, giving a low curtsey. She then slipped on her garden shoes and went out to refill all of the feeders in Bird Paradise, the haven Lorna had set up in her backyard for her feathered friends. The weather was certainly turning to spring, but with the chilly mornings, Martha figured the birds could use some ready-to-eat breakfast.

Routine completed, her mind came back to Ana's earlier call. Even though she'd solved the mystery of Aunt Lorna's debts, Martha still hadn't figured how to get out from under them. She had the writers' retreat, her new online business, and hopefully the contract with Ana to count on, but she was still unsure of when she'd feel the financial confidence she had enjoyed when she'd had a "real job" working for a college back in Boston.

Once again, the doubts set in. Had she made the right decision to stay here in Riley Creek, or was she going to have to throw in the towel?

Aboard the packet ship Mayfair, Atlantic Ocean, May 20, 1890

I WRITE THIS PASSAGE by the light of the blessed sun, a sight we have seen little of these past weeks. Our journey to Boston was to have taken us two weeks, but thanks to gales the Lord has brought upon us, we have extended that time by a good seven days. Our Captain tells us we are within three days of spying land, and I pray he is correct in his prediction.

I was well-prepared for my journey and knew when boarding that the ship carried primarily mail and cargo, with human cargo something of an afterthought. My brother, bless him, saw to it that I was booked along with fifteen to twenty others into a section just below the deck so that we have access to fresh air on occasion, but even these kinder quarters have begun to reflect smells that I dare not record here. God help those wretches who have spent their journey in steerage deeper below! I have heard their cries most keenly on days of rough seas, though they do not emerge to take air on deck as we do.

I share my cabin with a Londoner. While I have spent most days reading books about the flora and fauna of my future home, my fellow passenger has made ample use of the saloon on board, most days drinking far more than his fill. I know not what he has made of my daily prayer, but I attest that I have never once seen him kneel throughout our time together.

Our cabin is small and was reasonably equipped when we boarded with a set of linens to last the journey, a thin mattress and a washbasin, which we share. We receive fresh water for our washing two times per week. The cabin opens directly to an area with a long table where we take meals together, the Captain joining us most evenings for dinner. Food has been passable, but now that our journey has been extended by so many days, the fare has become more meager and the tea more watery.

As much as I counted the minutes until we set sail, just two days into our journey, I came to realize how slowly a day can pass when I am not traveling, visiting, or accompanying Mother on errands. Many of my compatriots are strong conversationalists, it is true, but their interests and mine rarely intersect. A few are students, going abroad to expand their experiences or to visit family who have emigrated. Most of the other men are entrepreneurs, confident that they can capitalize on trade opportunities. I am but a second son, in search of a place where I may be my own man and create my own destiny.

The first few days, I eagerly shared my vision for the future with a few of the other gentlemen seated at the dinner table, but realized from their furrowed brows and even a few jokes made at my expense that they thought little of my plan to join a community of equals. They cannot seem to understand my enthusiasm for building a place better than the one I left, where birth order does not form the basis of one's possibilities in life. But why should they understand? Few of these men face the same dilemma as I, already holding land themselves or being otherwise content to be supported by another's means.

I have held myself somewhat away from the others since these early conversations, staying in my cramped room or on deck to read or write in this journal, and only joining the bonhomie of my fellow passengers at mealtimes. The scrutiny of others has not dulled my excitement to reach Boston and, from there, to travel south to Tennessee to the place I will soon call home: New Canaan. I will endeavor to keep a faithful record of my new beginning.

Chapter Two

The next morning, after taking Penny on a short jog along the river and providing her with the pats and scratches to which she was entitled, Martha showered, dried her short brown hair, threw on her fleece vest and backpack, and headed out. Letting the screen door bang behind her, she stood for a beat in the early spring sun hitting the front porch. There was still enough of a bite in the air to warrant an extra layer, but the sun held the promise of warmer weather to come.

"When do those writers arrive?" she heard Delores Ritzen-waller yell from her own front porch where she sat in an Adirondack chair, sipping coffee. Delores had been one of Martha's aunt's closest friends. She was a part-time librarian who enjoyed puttering around in her *Southern Living*-caliber yard. Her caramel-colored German Shepherd Fritz sat at her side, pretending to be relaxed, yet Martha knew he was every bit on alert.

"Tomorrow," Martha cupped her hand at her mouth and yelled back. "Wish me luck at the R-C!" Delores gave a wave and a thumbs-up, and Martha headed down the stairs and toward the square.

The meeting was to be held at Toad in a Hole so that the whole group could see what Octavius Bennett, its transplanted British proprietor, had done in preparation for the retreat. As Martha approached the shop, she glanced over her shoulder to take in the hanging baskets suspended from every light pole ringing the square. Each moss-lined basket held a bright orange petunia surrounded by clouds of purple lobelia, ivy tumbling over the edges and hanging down. Delores, who had designed and assembled the many pots, had taught Martha her killer combo move: thriller (center plant), filler (surrounding plants) and spiller (some kind of ivy or vine). The effect was stunning, and it gave the square an added touch of charm.

Looking down the length of the square, Martha saw the *Welcome, Writers!* sign that Frank Elder had hung above the door of his hardware shop. Small groupings of chairs and tables were scattered under the cover of the square's towering oak trees to create cozy places to converse, daydream or write.

They won't be able to say we didn't roll out the red carpet! Martha reflected as she pushed on the door of Toad in a Hole and caused the brass bell hanging from the doorknob to tinkle.

Once she'd waved to the assembled retailers, Martha stopped to actually take in the bookshop's transformation. Sun streamed in through the sail-shaped floor-to-ceiling stained-glass window that made up most of the back wall. Ladders were attached to tracks that ran the length of the bookshelves on either side of the store, but today, the ladders were pushed all the way to the ends and hung suspended near the rear of the shop. The display tables that usually held stacks of new books had disappeared and in their place stood over a dozen table and chair combos. Easy chairs whose cushions held the general shapes of hundreds of behinds had been dotted carefully around the hardwood floor. Martha recognized a few from Birds 'n' Beans, some (she thought) from the library, and others must have been donated for the occasion by people in the village. Each table sported a cup with pens and pencils, a legal pad, and either a stress ball of some kind or a Fidget Spinner.

In the center of the room stood a strange contraption that looked like it had been stolen from the bridge of the U.S.S. *Enterprise*. A four-foot-high black plastic post on wheels, it had a cord running from its base to a plug in a floor outlet.

Octavius hurried over, excitedly smoothing his comb-over. He was dressed in a brighter-than-usual purple argyle sweater vest, white shirt, khaki pants and New Balance tennis shoes, and his glasses were perched just on the tip of his nose. Martha was relieved to see they were attached to a cord that ran around his neck.

"Welcome, *El Presidente*!" he said, holding his arms up in the air. There was a smattering of applause from the fifteen or twenty people—Martha guessed at the number rather than counting—who were in attendance and she gave a small wave, calling out a general greeting to the group.

"This looks amazing, Octavius!" she said, gesturing around at the converted bookstore space.

"Our own bestselling author was most helpful to me in placing the tables, based on what she said she would find comfortable as a writer. Ah! There she is." Octavius waved to Margaret Goodman, who was standing shyly in the back of the shop. Margaret, a retired high school English teacher, had surprised them all (except for Octavius, who'd been in on the secret) by publishing a steamy romance novel last fall. It had been met with critical acclaim—*whatever critical acclaim even means in the world of borderline erotica*, Martha wondered, not for the first time. Dressed in her usual black Chuck Taylors, Margaret had added black leggings, a black skirt, black corduroy shirt and black fleece jacket to complete her ensemble. She flushed crimson and waved back to Octavius.

He turned back to Martha and explained that he wanted Toad in a Hole to be a drop-in center for the upcoming nature writers' retreat. Gesturing expansively around the space, he said, "This is the place that any retreat participant can come to unplug and read"—here, he pointed to the comfy chairs by the window—"or plug in"—here, he gestured at the odd sci-fi tower Martha had noticed earlier, and she now saw a number of outlets running up and down its sides—"and write when their muse emerges." By now, Octavius was pink in the face, so tickled was he with what he and Margaret had been able to produce in the somewhat limited space.

"Octavius, it's amazing. I'm sure the writers will appreciate all the trouble you've gone to," Martha said, squeezing his arm. After a pause, she added, "If it's OK, I'd like to go ahead and start the meeting."

"Certainly, certainly," he replied, motioning for those clustered in small groups around the room to find a seat. One by one, they settled either at a writer's table or into the comfy chairs, and looked expectantly at Martha.

"Good morning, everyone," Martha said, feeling spring butterflies in her stomach. "Welcome to the third meeting of the R-C. Today, I'd like to run through the weekend's events and make sure that everything is ready for the writers' arrival. I'd like to thank our secretary Lew for taking notes, and his mom Cat for supplying us with coffee and rolls for this meeting."

Lewis Shipman held up his tablet and gave a thumbs-up, and Cat beamed.

"Ready for the Queen of France's arrival, more like," said Dan Montgomery, owner of the Piggly Wiggly over in Adair. A few nods.

Ethel Jean, co-owner of Silent Sisters Antiques that adjoined Birds 'n' Beans, called out vigorously, "Piggly Wiggly there said it right. We're just high-tech prostitutes for these artsy-fartsies."

Cat shook her head at Dan, and then looked around the room, arm held up. "Hey, folks," she said. "I don't know about you all, but I know An Early Riser sure could use the business these folks can bring. All the time between the blizzard and when a few tourists finally started finding us again really hit us hard."

Mumbled agreement.

"Be sure you get that in the minutes, honey," Cat told her son.

Clint the barber looked sheepishly up at Martha. "It does seem like we've had to work awful hard to get ready for a bunch of people who are probably going to hole up in their cabins with their computers and call it a day. I mean, we all appreciate what you've done, Martha, but... well, I dunno." He crossed his arms and pressed his lips together.

"Hey, folks, listen up." Don Chelton—Ranger from Paris State Park and married to Helen, the birdiest person at Birds 'n' Beans—stood. "The park's in the red with all we've had to spend to rebuild some of the public restrooms and most of the riverside cabins after all of the winter storm damage. Anything we can do to get folks coming back up here to our beautiful spot in the woods, we oughta do it."

Helen nodded and said, "People have lots of options for their spring tourism, so we're lucky Martha was able to get this group to agree to come up here, especially after the, ah, events over the winter. Pretty sure Jason would agree with me, if he wasn't *already* up in the mountains for the next week with an early trout group, trying to make up for lost revenue."

Do you mean events like the blizzard and the dead guy? Martha thought cynically. Then she cleared her throat. Helen was on her side. And Jason Turngate, owner of Fins to Fur in the village square, had certainly suffered more losses than most during the winter storm when a tree had fallen on his outdoors store.

"Everyone, I know this has been a lot of work and expense. I know it was difficult to put together the various welcome gifts and discounts for your shops, and I know the spiffing up and decorating we've all been doing has been time-consuming. But my hope is that if we spend a little, we'll be able to make up for early in the year when most of us had to be closed. The not-insignificant registration fees the writers paid will cover their lodging and the events we've planned for them. Anything they spend beyond that is income for Riley Creek businesses."

She paused and, hearing no disagreement, plowed forward. "Let's run through what we've got planned."

The next few minutes were spent discussing the weekend's events. Writers would start arriving tomorrow and the retreat would officially open with a keynote and dinner in the church-turned-community-center. The rest of the long weekend featured nature walks, readings, yoga and other wellness sessions, and plenty of empty spaces for writing time at Toad in a Hole, Birds 'n' Beans, or any other spot the workshop participants chose. The merchants' hope, of course, was that the writers would pass at least some of their time visiting the local shops and spending their money.

As they reached the end of the event schedule and were discussing the closing ceremony, Mary Jane Noel, retired nurse, sister to Ethel Jean and co-owner of Silent Sisters, rushed into the shop, accompanied by Alexis Bloom, owner of the Ohm Mama yoga studio that had recently reopened in Riley Creek. Mary Jane was finishing off what looked to have been a chocolate cupcake.

"Oh sheesh, Scarlett O'Hara making her grand entrance." Ethel Jean's unmistakable wry commentary came from somewhere in the crowd.

"Sorry, sorry! So sorry, everyone!" Mary Jane said. Alexis took off her cross-body bag and found a seat in the back of the shop while Mary Jane capped her chocolate milk jug and stowed it in a knit bag that hung almost to her knees. She wore a long pink cotton duster over a Namaste! yoga shirt and capri-length spandex pants.

"I'm sorry we're late," Mary Jane panted, remaining standing near Martha. "Yoga class ended a little late."

Martha noticed Alexis redden a bit, and then Ethel Jean said, "Yeahhh. And bats are flying out of my belfry. I notice it didn't end so late you didn't have time to go get one of Carl's cupcakes."

"Chocolate contains *protein* and *protein* is good for recovery," a smiling Mary Jane said in a singsong voice.

"Yeah. Recovery from eating so much *chocolate*, more like."

A titter rippled through the shop. Everyone was used to these two sisters and their sometimes-friendly-and-sometimes-not bickering.

Mary Jane looked down at the trusty Timex she wore, a reminder of her former vocation. "I know you're probably wrapping up, but I wanted to report that I was finally able to pin down the arrival time for our opening evening keynote speaker. I must say that she's been... challenging to work with, but her agent and I have sorted it all out and everything is now set. I think."

Martha felt instant relief. Carla Innsbruck was the big draw, and she hoped this famous name would attract more visitors than just the writers already in town for the retreat to the opening evening keynote.

Maybe things are going to work out just fine after all.

New Canaan, Tennessee, United States, June 15, 1890

WE ARRIVED AT A WHARF in Boston where I was greeted by Mr. Armstrong, a member of the Boston and London Mutual Aid Society. I was a bit chagrined as I made my way from the boat, given that we'd been short on fresh water the last few days of the journey, but Mr. Armstrong was quite amenable and helped me find my way out of the city's raucous and overly populated North End, where I understand many of my shipmates from steerage were bound.

How like London was Boston! Horses, children, every kind of sweet and fabric shop you can imagine, and even electric trollies lumbering by. It was a sight to behold! As in London, a cacophony of voices met my ears. I caught a few Scottish voices, but also Irish, German, Italian and even some languages of the East that I could not identify. While I was full of the excitement of the sights and sounds of this new city, I could not help but notice many men huddled at the bases of buildings, looking bereft of food and shelter. Such a strange sight amidst so much industry.

Mr. Armstrong explained that, while so many had been coming here over the last several decades and so many stayed in the city, this part of Boston was merely a stopping point to other occupations beyond the city center. There, mills, railways and other industries had expanded the reach of Boston quite significantly. Alas, my time with Mr. Armstrong was short, just a walk and a wonderfully restorative meal, and then he delivered me to what was to be my home for the next many weeks: a buggy pulled by two horses and a taciturn driver named Thompson. As much as I wish to report I took a train to my destination, most train expansions were heading toward the western states and not south as I was bound.

I won't belabor the next several days' journey; suffice to say that Thompson and I slept rough for most of it, he uttering more syllables to the horses than to me, and I so full of the sights and sounds of this new country that the fellow's rudeness barely concerned me. We moved from city to city: New Haven, New York, Philadelphia, Roanoke. Some cities boasted developed roads while others seemed to hold little more than dirt pathways. President Harrison, I think, has much to accomplish in this part of his country.

At last, we arrived in New Canaan. And what a sight it was! The gentle slopes of Virginia are no comparison to the hills of Tennessee. Every kind of tree you can imagine, groups of deer and turkey in numbers I have never observed. Fields of spring flowers lie between hills rolling away toward breathtaking blue mountains that, early in the morning, are embraced by the clouds. The heat is oppressive—such that I have never experienced, even during a London August—and mosquitoes are thick in the evenings. Those I can periodically escape, whereas the heat I cannot.

As I write this, I am at the small New Canaan Inn, the only guest house here, preparing for a much-needed bath. Thompson is due to head out tonight, so I shall share one more silent dinner with him, pay him his remainder, and wish him well. My adventure begins in earnest tomorrow.

Chapter Three

Once the R-C meeting had broken up, Martha stuck around to drink coffee with some of the members, even though she desperately wanted to get to the shop and check to see if any online orders had come in. Thanks to Margaret and Joanne, she now had a spanking-new website for the Fly Buy Beans brand, but so far, only a few orders. She had hoped those few orders would automatically become hundreds more, but regardless of how many times she refreshed the page, the site wasn't getting traffic.

She knew from shadowing her ex-boss and college president that spending time with people was an important part of being a new leader. She was determined to do a good job with the role she had been given, even though she hadn't really had a burning passion to lead the R-C. Pouring herself a glass of ice water from a pitcher, she walked over to where Clint and Alexis were gathered in a circle with Tara Jackson, owner of the Looking Sharp beauty salon. As soon as Martha drew close, Clint stopped gesturing animatedly and dropped his voice. As she joined them, Alexis flushed, seeming embarrassed to have been caught listening to Clint.

"Hi, all," Martha said breezily. "What'd I miss?"

"Clint here was trying to convince us that all the work we've been doing was for nothing and that this whole writers' conference is one big, bad idea," said Tara. She stood a full head taller than most of the others in the room, sporting long dreadlocks, Birkenstock clogs and a linen tunic matched with wide, flowy pants.

Clint sputtered. "Well, it's nothing against you, Martha; it's just that after the bad winter, I'm down to fumes on my checking account, if you get my drift."

"I get it, Clint, I really do. And I understand that you can only do so much to help. But honestly, anything you can do to contribute to the weekend is appreciated. We're hoping it brings in business for all of us, or at least gives us some great word-of-mouth advertising for the future."

Tara nodded and said, "I think Martha's onto something with this retreat. When I practiced corporate law a lifetime ago, my clients always swore they had to spend money to make money. I'm not sure what we're hosting is on the same scale as a multi-million-dollar marketing blitz, but I have a good feeling about it."

Alexis looked up at the taller woman. "*You* were in corporate law? I knew you had a different job before you opened the salon, but I guess I didn't realize *how* different. How in the heck did you end up in Riley Creek doing nails and skin?"

"Sure was. In uptown Manhattan for twenty-five years. How I ended up here is a long, long story, but suffice to say it's the best move I ever made."

"My folks helped me buy the business once Mavis... was no longer able to run it. They're helping me finance the new building. Nothing mysterious here," Alexis said airily. "Owing so much to the bank definitely is stressful, though, so I kinda get where Clint's coming from." She shot an apologetic glance at Martha.

Tara put her long arms around Clint and Alexis's shoulders. "As I say to my clients who are getting their first Brazilian, 'Ya' gotta trust the process.'"

Mary Jane pulled Martha away just as Clint was getting the lowdown on what a 'Brazilian' was. "Put wax on your *WHAT*?" she heard him say as she was led over to the corner.

"So, here's the thing," Mary Jane said to Martha, as if they'd already been mid-conversation. "Carla Innsbruck is somewhat... challenging to deal with. I've been working with her agent, Sherry Newcomb, who is very nice, but I just wanted you to know that Carla doesn't get out much, so is a bit of a... character. I think it'll all go fine tomorrow, but wanted to give you a heads up since you'll be introducing her."

"So, we've invited someone to be our keynote who is difficult and doesn't spend time around other people? Oh, GREAT!" Martha felt the eyes in the room turn in their direction. In a lower tone, she hissed, "Oh, *great*! Were you *at least* able to get a bio I can use?"

"Sherry said that Carla is a bit sensitive about people introducing her. See, it's been a while since she's done any public speaking and she's a bit... shy."

"Mary Jane! You said this woman was perfect for the keynote, that she'd draw a huge crowd and you had an 'in' with her! Now you're saying our featured speaker, our big chance to sell tickets and make some money, is *SHY*?"

Mary Jane pulled Martha out of the shop and onto the sidewalk.

"I do think she'll be a big draw since she hasn't made a public appearance in about... five years. See, before she went to jail after splashing pigs' blood all over a federal facility, she'd been a prolific environmental writer and activist. Her activism just... happens behind the four walls of her cabin up in the mountains these days. She hasn't published since going to jail, doesn't ever go out in public and has become a bit of a recluse, apparently."

Martha simmered in silence.

Mary Jane continued, "But think of some of the great reclusive writers. Harper Lee. Emily Dickinson. This could be the keynote of the century, getting a recluse and activist to come to *our* nature writers' retreat!"

"And just what is this 'in' you have with her? I'm an idiot for not having asked that question much sooner."

"A contractor that worked on her roof came into Frank's store," Mary Jane replied in a small voice, the end of her sentence rising as if a question.

Martha held her head in her hands and squeezed her eyes closed. Mary Jane kept talking.

"Sherry *assured* me she'd have Carla here and ready to roll for the keynote, and that she is *sure* Carla will be a very engaging speaker. Those are the words she used. *Very*. *Engaging*. She just has to be handled with kid gloves, that's all."

"Wait a minute... if she's such a recluse, why did she decide to speak at our event?" Martha asked, pulling her head back up to a normal position.

"According to Sherry, Carla has strong feelings about the proposed development over in Riverton and sees this as a chance to speak out about it. Plus, she needs the small honorarium we were able to scrape together," she added, looking up at the sky as if assessing the chance of rain.

"If I didn't love you, I think I'd kill you right now," Martha said, sighing and checking her watch. "But it's too late to go to a plan B now. This is the Riley Creek Nature Writers' Retreat, she's all about saving the environment, and she is a writer. I guess we just pray it all works out the way we need it to."

That afternoon, Martha had promised, she and Teddy would go on a date since the next several days were likely to be busy for both of them. They'd not seen each other much in the weeks and months following the blizzard. Martha had been working with Ana on the upcoming contract for coffee, as well as reading up on how to establish a successful online business. In the early weeks following the storm, business at Birds 'n' Beans had been blessedly steady as she, PJ and Helen had served coffee and lunch to the many utility crews, insurance adjusters, and repair people who'd streamed in.

Being the sole coffee shop in an out-of-the-way location has its advantages, Martha had thought, more than once. But the repair people had all gone home and Martha was back to the same old question she'd been mulling over for weeks. Few people outside Riley Creek had ever heard of her shop, so how could she draw them to it over the internet?

The "date" that afternoon was actually lunch at Teddy's house. Not for the first time, she took in the orderly box yews lining the crazy paving walkway and the symmetrical flowerbeds with cleanly sculpted borders. She thought of Aunt Lorna's beautiful cottage garden and the weeds that were beginning to sprout like unsightly chin hairs. Reflexively, her hand came up to inspect her own chin at the same time that she rang the bell with her other hand.

The door opened and there was Teddy, black haired and bronze skinned thanks to his Italian grandfather. Martha flushed as she took in his six foot two frame, khakis and dress shirt with the sleeves rolled up.

Teddy leaned down to kiss her on the cheek and said, "Come on in. I'm just about to put lunch on the table." Easing past him and into the house, she took in his familiar scent of pine and woodsmoke.

Yum.

The few times she'd been over had been enough for him to prove what a great cook he was, and also reinforced that Martha's culinary strengths were limited to heating coffee beans in the ancient Royal roaster in the shop. Today when she arrived at his small ranch house, he was busy spreading pesto on two ciabatta rolls, layering sundried tomatoes, turkey, and provolone cheese, and cutting each sandwich diagonally into two pieces. Martha groaned inwardly as she looked over at the dining nook, which had been carefully laid with a flowered tablecloth, striped linen napkins, and colorful Fiestaware, all in fiery reds and golds. She knew that if she'd tried to pull off something like that, it would just look like someone had spilled ketchup and mustard all over the table.

They chatted over their sandwiches, Teddy catching her up on the meager happenings at the station. Things had calmed down quite a bit since the events of December, giving him a chance to settle into his new job as chief of police. Martha chattered on about the shop, feeling jittery and distracted.

"So, have you thought anymore about my invitation?" Teddy asked, wiping his mouth with a napkin.

"What invitation?" Martha asked, knowing full well which invitation he meant. Teddy was silent. "Oh, *that* invitation." Martha blinked innocently. "I'm still thinking on it. Things have been so busy at the shop, and now we've got the retreat... I just haven't had a minute to myself."

Teddy leaned against the back of his chair. "Why do I have the feeling you're procrastinating? What's so hard about just saying yes?"

Martha shifted uneasily, feeling trapped on her side of the suddenly very small eating area. "I don't know. I... I'm just not sure it's a great time to be away from the shop when we've got so much going on."

"It's not even the height of birding season, Martha. And your team can handle you being gone for three whole days. When's the last time you actually took a day off?"

"Business owners don't take days off. It's different for you."

He visibly tensed. "So it's *easier* for me to be away, is that what you're saying?"

"No, no, that's not what I mean." Martha felt her irritation grow. "It's just... I feel... I'm not sure about the whole romantic getaway and meeting your daughter thing. I mean, you and I are still getting to know each other. I'm not sure I'm ready for all that."

Teddy's voice grew softer. "It's a weekend away to hike and enjoy ourselves. No strings attached. And seeing my daughter... well, that's part of getting to know me, Martha. She's my *daughter*."

"I know, I know. I'm thinking on it. I just..." She stood up, wiping her mouth and placing her napkin on the edge of the table. "Look, thanks for lunch. It was delicious. I really have to get going."

With that, she headed out the front door and didn't look back.

She drove over the speed limit to get to Birds 'n' Beans. Parking her Subaru in the shop's lot around back, Martha entered through the back door. As she passed them, she noticed that the feeders in the viewing garden were looking low on seed.

"Hey, guys!" she yelled, tossing her backpack behind the counter. "I'm going out to fill the feeders."

She walked over to a heavy-duty outdoor storage box, opened it, and began to scoop seed using an old Tupperware pitcher. Behind her, situated outside the glass back wall of the shop, was the treed courtyard where, several years before, her Aunt Lorna had designed a small viewing garden, which featured multiple bird feeding stations. Using the wild bird blend seed, Martha filled the tubes and platform feeders. Next, she filled the thistle bags with nyger seed (goldfinches would be going mad for it at this time of year), and lastly, she pulled fresh squares of nutrient-rich suet out to place into specially shaped feeders. Martha knew from Helen that, even though birds could find more food sources in the early spring than in winter, it helped migrating species if they could pick up a quick snack on the way to their destination.

Once the feeders were full, Martha closed the storage box up and headed back inside. The scent of roasting spice and chocolate hit her full force as she crossed the threshold. Martha never tired of taking in the wall of feeders and birdhouses, pallets of seed, glass case of binoculars, and displays of bird-themed gifts, or the collection of mismatched chairs and tables in the center of the store that looked out onto the viewing garden. It all brought her Aunt Lorna back so vividly that she couldn't help but smile.

The place was buzzing, making her smile even wider. PJ was working the espresso machine and Helen was restocking the shelves of bird checklists near the front door. Margaret occupied one of the tables and, from the look of her ferocious typing, she must have been cranking out her current bodice-ripper.

Helen turned and waved to Martha. "Sorry the feeders were so low. A delivery came in this morning so I'm a bit behind on things here."

"No sweat." Martha consulted her watch. "The first writers should start trickling in fairly early tomorrow. Is everything ready for check-in as far as you know?"

"Yep. Dot has the day off from the flea market, and she and Nathan will arrive at the camp store first thing to help with check-in for the cabins. Each cabin has an itinerary inside and we'll tell each guest to relax until dinner and the keynote, which will both be happening at the church. Ex-church. Community center. Ummmm..."

PJ chimed in from behind the counter. "I think we settled on community center, since it's no longer holding religious services. Delores and Jimmy will be there to receive all the crockpots of chili that are being donated for tomorrow night."

Since Pastor Pat and his wife Ellie had moved away and the "church chumps" (as Ethel Jean called the regional church leadership) had decided not to replace him, the First Methodist Church had stood empty. Joanne kept an eye on the building and had gotten the church's permission to use the space as a community center as long as it was kept clean and maintained. So far, it had proven a mutually beneficial arrangement. The R-C, in planning for the retreat, had decided that it would be perfect for the kickoff and keynote the next evening.

"Fantastic. Sounds like everything is humming. Do you gals mind if I check in on the online shop and see if we've gotten any activity?"

"Wait a sec! Wait!" PJ untied her apron, this one featuring Bigfoot wearing a Love is Love t-shirt and making the shape of a heart with his two hairy hands. Reaching under the counter, she brought out a slender book and held it out.

Online Sales for Absolute Dummies.

"Now, honey, I know that title is a bit off-putting. But we've got to start somewhere if we're going to get Fly Buy Beans off the ground. I've already finished Chapter One and I've learned that we have to have snappy images of our coffees to share on social media. So I'm going to start taking lots of pictures." Here, she pulled her phone from her pocket. "Joanne is going to help me make us a Facebook page, and she says I can put my pictures there." She held up her phone and toggled it into photo mode. "Smile, everyone!"

Helen, PJ and Martha clustered together so PJ could take a group selfie. At that precise moment, Ethel Jean came through the hallway that connected Silent Sisters Antiques to Birds 'n' Beans, walked behind the threesome and held up her middle finger as the phone whirred and captured the image.

New Canaan, Tennessee, United States, July 16, 1890

I HAVE SCARCELY HAD time to write since my arrival in New Canaan a little over one month ago. I've promised myself to try to be more faithful to my diary, yet I find that from the moment I awake until the moment I lay my head down, there is little time for anything resembling regular entries.

Life here moves so very fast, but I will do my best to summarize all that has happened since I last wrote in these pages. New Canaan was established six months ago, so there was already a small group of families, a handful of second and third sons, and a smattering of others here when I arrived. All have come from cities and towns around England, ready, as I am, to make a new start. A few Londoners are here who feel that the city has simply grown too large and they want to live somewhere with fewer slum dwellings.

Most American New Canaanites come from the northeast United States, men and women whose home professions have been taken over by factories. Our own English textile companies exported the notion of mechanized work some years ago, and it sounds as if the concept has been applied to many other industries. While production has certainly increased, these people's stories of working for twelve hours on a shop floor are almost too horrible to recount here. I'm told there have been some labor uprisings in past years and I have no doubt that, based on the stories I've heard, they will continue.

Though we all came here with different stories to tell, the men and women of New Canaan have in common many dreams and aspirations. A nail machine operator who works from sunup to sundown for a pittance has the same empty pockets as a third son with no land and no prospects. Here, with the help and generosity of our mutual aid friends, our plan is to carve out additional farm fields and eventually feed ourselves and turn a profit such that we can expand our community. Individually, we have few resources, but together, we believe we can do better.

Even now, a man has come from Boston to plan the roads and public buildings, taking lessons from other cities and towns so that we might avoid the worst of their mistakes. The truest excitement for us, which fires us in the midst of long days clearing fields of rocks, is the promise of a rail line connecting New Canaan to the nearby central line. By the time New Canaan's crops are on a regular rotation of production, we will be able to take them on a train to sell for profit in nearby cities.

I have made many friends here, but just one who might be called my closest friend. His name is Thomas Hoffmann and he is from Germany. Though he does not speak much of his family, I gather that he and they settled in Cincinnati a few years ago, but that, like me, he chose to take a different path from the shoemaker future his father had chosen for him. But I see from the look in his eyes when he speaks of them—and particularly his sister, Susannah—that he feels their absence most keenly when the days are long.

The best times for us are when we join the whole community for swimming in the ice-cold river or to raise a building and enjoy a picnic lunch afterward. Of course, the VERY best times are when some of the older men travel back with Pilsener from the Memphis Brewing Company. Thomas complains that American beer tastes like water, but still he manages to drink his fill.

The days are long, the work is harder than I ever imagined, but still it is preferable to the second-class existence I was destined for in

England. I look forward to the day when I can report in these pages that I have truly established myself. I expect that will not happen for a few years, but my hope and faith are strong.

Chapter Four

The next day, shop customers had gotten sparse by the end of the afternoon. Dot, a friend of Don's and manager of the Green Maples Flea Market, had volunteered to help check in the writers, and had just texted Martha to say that the last one had arrived. PJ had offered to cover both Birds 'n' Beans and Silent Sisters so that Martha, Helen, and Ethel Jean could go hear the keynote address—apparently, the selfie photo-bomb situation had sorted itself out, and PJ and Ethel Jean were friends again. Mary Jane and Frank were going to meet the group at the community center.

"If those two spent as much time running their businesses as they do making out in the back of the hardware shop, there might actually be some profits coming into this town," Ethel Jean growled on the way out the door. The three piled into Martha's car and made a quick stop at the cottage to pick up Penny. One side of her beard was completely flat, evidence that she'd slept the whole day away.

"Come on, silly girl," Martha called to the terrier. "With any luck, you might bump into Chip or Fritz," Chip being Allison's Golden Retriever.

Once Penny had left a few messages around the front yard and mailbox for fellow canines, she hopped into the back and settled on Ethel Jean's lap. Ethel Jean harrumphed, but Martha noticed out of the corner of her eye that the older woman's age-spotted hand rested on Penny's back for the duration of the short drive.

As they reached the community center, memories of her emergency search grid during the winter's blizzard flashed through Martha's mind. As she took in the number of cars and trucks parked in the lot, however, she quickly grew excited at the thought of the tickets that might have been sold for the evening's festivities. She recognized Octavius's chalkboard sign atop an easel near the door, announcing in colorful letters, "Welcome to the First Annual Riley Creek Nature Writers' Retreat!" Someone (she guessed Delores) had artfully hung grapevine around the sign, giving it a rustic feel. At the large front doors, tall floral arrangements matching those in the hanging baskets on the square confirmed Delores's handiwork.

Martha led Penny to the enclosed yard behind the church, promising to pick her up after the festivities, then ran back around to the entrance. Joanne and Albert Jeremiah were selling dinner tickets from behind a table draped in a white tablecloth and topped with a Mason jar of spring flowers.

"*Bonjour, mes amis!*" exclaimed Joanne excitedly. She'd evidently selected peacock as the evening's theme, sporting a green tunic with the bird's distinctive feathers designed all over it and a chunky silver bracelet with a prominent "eye" as its centerpiece. A turquoise silk scarf with matching feathers graced her neck. The overall effect was stunning, if a bit much on the eyes.

"I can't believe this turnout!" said Helen. "There must be fifty or sixty cars parked out there."

"I'm just relieved we made extra chili and stocked the freezer last week," Martha replied, trying to modulate her own pride at the exceptional turnout.

In the Fellowship Hall, red-and-white checked tablecloths covered round tables that each held a Mason jar flower arrangement.

Crockpots lined the counter that ran along the side of the room. Once Martha and the others had mingled and greeted some of the guests, they sat down to enjoy chili, fresh cornbread, chocolate cupcakes and ice-cold sweet tea.

Mary Jane and Frank joined them midway through the meal.

"She's here. She's *here*," said Mary Jane breathlessly. "She and Sherry are in the vestry doing some last preparations."

"What's she like?" Martha asked.

"Well, I don't actually know," Mary Jane said, a bit haltingly. "Sherry said Carla didn't want to speak to anyone before her talk... and she doesn't really want to talk to anyone afterwards either. Even though, according to Sherry, just the marketing for this keynote has driven her existing book sales through the roof. She has quite the following."

"Quite an eclectic crowd," Frank observed. "Can you tell which ones are the writers?"

"I can't," said Martha, "but their retreat agendas tell them to meet back here after the keynote, so we'll know then."

"Ya mean what a bunch of weirdos," Ethel Jean offered. "I've never seen so many grey man buns and hairy-legged old women in my life. Is this a geriatric hobbit convention and no one told me?"

Mary Jane quickly shushed her sister. "Now, Ethel Jean. To each his or her own. These ladies and gentlemen likely attended an environmental action or two themselves way back when and are here to remember those good old days."

Just as she finished speaking, Octavius walked to the center of the room and lightly tapped a partially drained glass of tea with a dinner knife. "Ladies and gentlemen, if I may ask you to please make your way into the main hall, our guest of honor will begin her keynote in five minutes."

Bringing up the rear as the crowd made its way into what Martha couldn't stop thinking of as the nave, she noticed that some were carrying dog-eared books and she could just make out Carla Innsbruck's name on several of their covers.

This woman must have been a big deal back in the day, thought Martha as she caught sight of Delores and Jimmy slipping around to re-enter the Fellowship Hall, she guessed to help with cleanup.

In the nave—or rather, the main hall—the decorating crew had outdone itself. Not only did the spring floral theme continue in the form of a large centerpiece atop the altar, but soft lights glowed in the wall sconces and a candle flickered on the piano positioned next to the lectern. Bluegrass music played from an invisible source. With the large electric ceiling fixtures off, the effect was soothing.

After Margaret had placed a small glass of water under the pulpit, and then nearly run down from the chancel to her front row seat, Octavius motioned to Martha to come to the front for the introduction. Martha did as asked, heart pounding, and managed to thank the Retailers' Collective and other volunteers for their hard work. Getting into her stride, she thanked everyone for coming, gave a special welcome to the writers in Riley Creek for the retreat, and then introduced Carla Innsbruck.

"Our speaker for this evening needs no introduction, but please allow me to say how excited we are to welcome her back after some years away from public speaking. Carla Innsbruck has stood up for the environment in both word and deed, and we are thrilled to have her with us to open the First Annual Riley Creek Nature Writers' Retreat. Following the keynote, you're encouraged to head over to Toad in a Hole to purchase one of her titles. Without further ado, I present to you, Carla Innsbruck!"

As the applause rang out, the door of the vestry opened and a woman emerged. Martha wasn't sure what she'd been expecting, but she had to exert some effort to keep surprise from registering on her face. The woman came forward, hand outstretched to shake Martha's, and mouthed "Thank you." Taking that as her sign to return to her seat, Martha walked down the few steps to the front pew and sat next to Margaret as Carla Innsbruck took her place at the pulpit-turned-podium.

Carla looked to be a bit over five feet tall, her silver hair shaped into a stylish and straight pixie cut that complemented a ruddy complexion, its smoothness only broken by laugh lines. She wore tapered black pants and a long grey belted shawl with a fringe around the bottom. A crisp white shell blouse shone under the shawl, and her jewelry was understated: a silver bracelet on each wrist and turquoise and silver bead necklace that fell to just above the V of the shawl. She wore simple black closed-toe wedge shoes. The overall effect made Martha think of a silver-haired Joan Baez.

This person spent time in jail after breaking into a federal facility?

Carla Innsbruck unfolded a sheaf of papers and a pair of bright red reading glasses, and began her speech.

"Good evening and thank you for that warm welcome. It is my pleasure to welcome you to the First Annual Riley Creek Nature Writers' Retreat. I'm honored to be this evening's keynote speaker and, before I begin, want to wish all of you a relaxing and productive weekend. May I see a show of hands so we can applaud those writers in the room who are attending the retreat?"

A smattering of hands went up, some confident and others hesitant. Mary Jane caught Martha's eye as they looked around the room, the older woman positively beaming.

No train wreck so far, Martha reflected.

"Writers are special people because we willingly pursue a solitary craft, one where we are our own worst critics. And that's before we even birth our pieces so that the public can deliver yet more criticism!" The crowd let out a gentle chuckle, then Carla went on to detail the joys and trials of the writer's life. "Writers are some of my favorite people. They are strong, resilient, and willing to adapt their craft based on new data. Think of what a wonderful world this would be if everyone were like that!"

Nods all around.

OK, I like it, Martha thought, feeling more encouraged by the moment.

"But nature writers in particular have a special responsibility. It's not enough for these authors to work their very hardest to produce an error-free and compelling text. Once they enter the public arena—which by definition, published authors do—they are compelled to translate their ideas into action. Believe me, when I went to federal prison for protesting deforestation, I had a long time to think on this, and it occurred to me, even those many years ago, that *writing* about protecting the Earth cannot be divorced from *acting* on nature's behalf. And that is what I have come here tonight to encourage you to do."

Martha felt herself tense. Up to this point, the keynote had been progressing along a more or less predictable path, commending the retreat attendees and building them up for a long weekend of writing and reflection. Where was Carla Innsbruck going with this? Was this going to be encouragement to attend a Save the Trees rally? An Earth Day celebration?

Keep it breezy, lady, Martha telepathically implored the woman. *You're a keynote speaker, not a politician.*

Carla had only been glancing at her notes up until now, but at this point, she began reading word for word, using her free hand to gesture for emphasis.

"Tonight, I am introducing a new kind of environmentalism, one that works *with* Mother Nature instead of against her. For decades, I and others have fought modern development and the environmental destruction that comes along with it. But then the U.S. government gave me the gift of time—which at the time did not seem like a gift—and I had the opportunity to reflect on how successful this approach has been. Think about it: Wendell Berry, Aldo Leopold, Rachel Carson, Michael Pollan, and so many others. They lit the way for us. They showed us how our mistakes were going to cost the planet. But yet, here we are. Our world population is exploding. Rivers are disappearing. Global temperatures are climbing. Hundreds of species are facing extinction. What we've been doing is *not working*. So, it's time to change the narrative."

Martha blinked. Not a peep came from the gathered crowd.

"What I am advocating tonight is a new paradigm that turns away from the old, a model that stops fighting and starts cooperating. Simply put, we allow evolution to take place. Think about it: eventually, there will be no green space, no fresh water, no fish in the seas, and temperatures will climb so high that only small parts of the Earth will be habitable. And those only for a finite time into the future. The Earth will eventually fall under the weight of what we've done to it. But—and here's the exciting part—with that fall will come the extinction of the human species. And once that final extinction event has taken place, the true evolution will commence. I ask you: do you want to delay the inevitable? Or do you want to be part of a true ecological revolution?"

People in the hall shifted uncomfortably in their pews. Martha and Margaret looked sidelong at one another, Martha seeing her own shock reflected in Margaret's kitty cat glasses.

I need to end this thing, Martha thought.

Just as Martha rose from her seat, Carla took a sip of water and said, "They say all politics is local. Join me next Thursday over in Riverton where we will launch the new *Let the Earth Go* movement. Let's *encourage* the county commissioners to rezone the land next to the Paris River State Park for commercial use. Help bring the reign of the homo sapiens to a close."

Martha zoomed to the podium and extended her hand to Carla, nodding as if the talk had come to its natural end and she was simply thanking another run-of-the-mill keynote speaker for her inspiring words. Applause was sparse as Carla made her way from the stage and back to the vestry.

"Ladies and gentlemen, thank you so much for attending our chili dinner and opening event for the Riley Creek Nature Writers' Retreat. Our keynote speaker was certainly... thought provoking. Don't forget to stop in at Toad in a Hole to pick up one of her titles. Writers, if you'll please make your way to the Fellowship Hall, we'll go over some logistics before adjourning for the evening."

Those assembled began to stand and walk to the back of the nave, but Martha couldn't miss some of the dirty glances that came her way and toward the door of the vestry where Carla had disappeared. She guessed that most of these folks had bought a ticket to get a glimpse of the old Carla Innsbruck, the same one who'd chained herself to the entrance of national parks, freed animals from campus labs in the dark of night, and, most famously, covered federal land management offices in pigs' blood, protesting the lack of action against deforestation. *This* Carla Innsbruck sounded like she'd gone around the bend after so many years in seclusion.

The main hall had emptied out, and Martha was relieved to see Albert and Joanne standing by the front doors, cheerily thanking the last guests for attending and handing particularly angry-looking individuals one of the floral centerpieces as they left. Most of the merchants and her friends who'd attended had headed back to town, Ethel Jean catching a ride with Octavius.

Martha, Helen, and Margaret made their way to the Fellowship Hall to meet the writers and review the weekend's agenda. Mary Jane stayed in the nave and moved toward the pulpit, Martha guessed to collect the water glass and bid their speaker and her agent goodbye. She decided to let Mary Jane deal with Carla Innsbruck while she did damage control with the writers.

She could see when she reached the Fellowship Hall that Delores and Jimmy had worked their magic so well that there was not one cornbread crumb visible on any of the tables. All eighteen of the writers were assembled, a few of them whispering among themselves and exchanging troubled glances. Martha decided to nip things in the bud.

"Well," she said airily, "if good keynotes are supposed to be provocative, ours certainly took the cake."

Helen took pity on her and stood with a copy of the agenda. First making sure everyone had one, she then ran through the weekend's events, answering various questions from writers as she went along. Then Margaret stood and described the setup at Toad in a Hole, emphasizing that the space would be open to the writers each day of the retreat from seven in the morning until eight in the evening.

Once all questions had been answered, the writers filed out, except for four who stayed around to chat, each one popping out of the Fellowship Hall at one time or another, Martha assumed to use the restroom. After a few minutes, Mary Jane popped in briefly to say she'd locked the front doors and to let her know if anyone needed to have them unlocked in order to exit. Now, she was going to put some items back into storage.

Margaret sidled up to Helen and Martha and said in a quiet voice, "My research into writers' retreats said it was important to network. I think that's what they're doing." She looked around the room, then made a note in a small spiral notebook she'd taken from her pocket.

"What are you writing?" Martha asked.

"Nothing really. I'm just curious about the habits of other writers. Since I don't know any other writers except, well, me." She pushed her glasses up with a well-practiced gesture.

Chatting with the four retreat attendees who had hung around, introducing herself and answering any questions, Martha guessed that they were all first-timers. One, Angie Bangor, was a thirty-something administrative assistant from Nashville who was contemplating an MFA in Creative Writing and had decided that a retreat could be a good way to test the waters.

"The keynote speaker was...kinda weird, if you don't mind my saying so," she said somewhat tentatively. Her deep bass voice took Martha by surprise, running counter to the young woman's petite figure and delicate gestures.

Martha waved her hand. "Oh, we thought it could be interesting to host her as a way to reintroduce her after so many years. Could be that she was shakier about being in public again than we'd imagined."

"Hmmm..." Angie said, not sounding convinced. "Well, I kind of asked other people what they thought and they agreed with me. She was *weird*."

Martha reflected that perhaps Angie needed to keep her opinions to herself and focus on her writing this weekend.

"I also asked around and people are wondering if the weekend will be worth the money, if this is how it's starting."

Well, aren't we just the little busybody, Martha griped silently.

"Friends, Romans, and countrymen, time for this guy to get some shuteye," another of the writers said as he re-entered the Fellowship Hall. Martha was grateful for the distraction, even if the cause of it did come across as a tad obnoxious. Nick Temple, who she'd overheard bragging to Helen about his successful nature photography career, wore tight-fitting Levis, a tight white t-shirt, and wingtip shoes that had seen better days. As he fit a strand of stray brown hair back into its ponytail, Martha reminded herself that though he seemed a bit of a blowhard, he was a *paying* blowhard.

Two other writers, a local woman named Liz Waterson and a Johnson City editor named Karen Todd, had been talking at another table. Karen sported a black cardigan over a black t-shirt and black jeans (*she could exchange fashion tips with Margaret*, Martha thought briefly) and Waterson looked like she'd walked out of an L.L. Bean catalog, all chinos and deck shoes and three-quarter-sleeved Oxford shirt. The two women nodded to Nick in agreement that it was time to call the evening to an end, and the whole group began making motions to leave.

As they walked through the corridor that opened into the main hall, Martha was surprised to see the front door wide open. The remaining writers shuffled out and into the parking lot, Margaret, Helen and Martha bringing up the rear.

"Didn't Mary Jane say something about locking the front door?" Helen asked.

"Yes, she did. It's odd that it's standing open like that," Margaret replied.

"Weird, but not a big deal, right?"

"No, I suppose not," Margaret said, covering a yawn with the back of her hand. "I am rather tired."

Helen invited Margaret to exit ahead of her. "Your chariot awaits, my dear friend and producer of adult literature."

Martha realized how exhausted she, too, felt. She was just about to file out behind her friends when out of the corner of her eye, she noticed the light on in the vestry.

"Just a sec, Mary Jane must still be tidying up in there. I'll get her so we can all leave together."

She hurried up the aisle, mounted the two stairs in one jump, and pushed open the vestry door.

"Mary Ja—" Martha's words were cut short. Carla Innsbruck was lying sprawled on the floor, eyes wide open and a knife buried in her stomach. And Mary Jane was leaning over her, hands covered in blood.

New Canaan, Tennessee, United States, September 20, 1890

WHEN I ARRIVED MONTHS ago, New Canaan was already in its infancy—no, perhaps it would be better to say it had reached its young adulthood. Indeed, it is hard for me to imagine what might have greeted my compatriots when they first arrived. Even now, though we have a mill on the river, several farmsteads, a larger structure that serves as both church and school, a general store, and several homes, we are still small. At last count, New Canaan held a modest 250 souls, but we grow by a few heads every month, it seems.

Mr. Hicks is our leader and we call him "Mr. Mayor." We say it in jest, but I see a tint of pride in his eyes when we do. He leads us well, encouraging us, welcoming the newest, and finding resources for those souls who arrive in poorer condition than even I. Thank goodness for the Ladies' Aid group that receives these poor souls and helps them with clothing and tools and finds them at least makeshift accommodations. Mr. Hicks inspires us with visions of the future, once our crops are thriving and the railway connection arrives. He tells us that the railway will arrive sometime next year, and that is inspiration enough for Thomas and me.

Although today New Canaan boasts its own small inn, Thomas and I were both offered tents just outside of town for temporary living. In a small clearing, there are around ten raised platforms with tall-beamed structures affixed atop them. Over each of these structures is slung a large piece of canvas, enough to sweep down and over a cot and wood chest. The Ladies' Aid group provided us each with a net to hang over the heads of our cot when we arrived and thank God, for the mos-

quitoes here are sent from Satan himself. Upon the jut of platform that is not covered with the canvas sits a chair and table. It is rough accommodation, to be sure, but enough to feel I have a home for the present time.

Thomas and I have rented out our services, assisting with farming and any construction needed. We lend our backs and in return learn new skills and make a bit of a wage. We are saving carefully so that we can build our own homes and begin our own farms soon. I have already decided to share the little money I brought with me from home with Thomas so that our homes will be larger than what we might otherwise afford. These months together, connected with shared purpose and shared isolation, have forged a brotherly bond between us.

Tomorrow, we begin a project which I admit makes me long for home and its tall walls filled with finely spined book after book. We will commence construction on the New Canaan Library in the square. It will be a solid structure and no doubt will provide hours of contemplation and education for our village and its children.

But before the first board has been nailed, I confess, I find myself dreaming of the day that we will replace this modest structure with something grander and more permanent. Mr. Carnegie is building libraries here and abroad that could hold our mercantile store twenty-five times over. Dare I dream that one day, we could replace the structure of wood that we are beginning tomorrow with something made of stone? A library like that would surely show that our dream of community has taken hold and become a reality. Perhaps it could be named after Mr. Hicks, the man who is holding this community together in the face of so many trials and tribulations.

Addendum: Thomas has received tragic news from home which will no doubt redouble our industry. In a letter dated some weeks earlier, he learned that his parents' flat, a cramped space over a tobacco *shop, had been destroyed in a fire. It was only because his sister Su-sannah had been kept late at work, washing pans at a nearby bakery, that she was spared. She writes to say that she has used the last of their parents' savings to book passage to Boston, and will from there find her way to New Canaan to join Thomas. Thomas is much preoccupied by this news, and while I grieve for his parents with him, I wonder what this changing tide has in store for us and our plans.*

Chapter Five

"Mary Jane!" Martha yelled. "What happened?"

"What happened?" Mary Jane parroted, gesturing down at Carla. "She's dead! I was just about to yell for help when you came in. I'd been organizing the storage closet down the hall and noticed a light on in here. I assumed Sherry and Carla had left it on. I came in to turn it out and found her here."

Martha took in Mary Jane's countenance more closely and noticed a brown smudge on her cheek.

"Mary Jane, were you getting into the extra cupcakes while Carla was in here getting murdered?" Then Martha berated herself inwardly. *Really? That's your key takeaway from this scene?* Shock, it seemed, manifested itself in the strangest ways.

Mary Jane paused, blinked, said, "You need to call the police. Now!" Then she bent back over Carla's still form.

Martha turned and ran to Helen and Margaret, who were still standing in the back of the church. The last of the writers, luckily, had already driven away from the parking lot. Blurting out the basics to them, she was relieved to see Margaret quickly pull out her cell phone and start dialing. Instructing Helen to close the front door and not let anyone besides the police enter, Martha ran back to the nave. When she entered the vestry this time, Mary Jane was sitting leaning against the wall, face pale and bloody hands hanging down over the tops of her knees.

"Can I get you anything?" Martha asked cautiously. "Are you OK?"

"No," said Mary Jane. "I just... just don't know what to say. I know it's shock, but I need a minute. You'd think after all those years as a nurse, I'd be used to seeing dead bodies, but I guess I thought the one I saw last winter would be the last. Maybe ever. I guess not."

A few more seconds went by and they heard sirens drawing close. Then Penny started to howl and bark from the yard in back. There was a commotion out in the hall and moments later, Officer Chip Daniels and Chief Teddy Perry arrived in the doorway.

The two men quickly took in the scene.

"What are you two doing in here?" Teddy bellowed. "Get away from the body!"

Martha, Officer Daniels and Mary Jane all cringed at his tone. Speaking evenly, but through gritted teeth, Teddy carried on.

"You've got to move away. This is a crime scene, a fact I would think the two of you would have some appreciation for by now." He gave a sidelong glance at his fellow officer, whose mouth was still hanging open. The other man clapped his mouth shut and assumed a properly stoic expression.

Teddy led Martha and Mary Jane to the Fellowship Hall while the paramedics hustled up the aisle with a stretcher topped with equipment bags.

Mary Jane was heading straight for the sink when Teddy yelled, "STOP!" She halted in her tracks and he added, "Which of you found her?"

Mary Jane said, "I did, but I was—"

"That means anything you have on your hands could be evidence. You have to come down to the station to let us collect your clothing and take other evidence samples."

Mary Jane looked taken aback, but nodded in agreement. The three of them had just sat down at one of the round tables when Officer Daniels walked in.

"Sir, may I have a private word, please?"

Teddy excused himself and stepped out of the room with Officer Daniels. Fewer than two minutes later, Teddy came back in and stood next to Martha and Mary Jane. He held a small evidence bag out to them.

"Ms. Noel, does this belong to you?"

"You know it does, Teddy. It's my Timex."

"Then I'm afraid I'll need to continue this conversation with you down at the station. Your watch was found in the victim's hand."

"Well, of course it was. You know I've worn a Timex with a second hand ever since my nursing days. Her agent asked if she could borrow a watch so that she wouldn't go over the time allotted to her for the keynote."

"I can't help but notice your wrist appears to have abrasions on it," Teddy replied.

Both Martha and Mary Jane looked down right away and saw that he was right. There were faint pink scratches on the wrist where Mary Jane customarily wore her Timex.

"I must have scraped it taking the watch off to give to Carla. Or when I was organizing the leftovers in the closet just a few minutes ago." The weakness of the explanation rang out even as they heard the stretcher rolling down the aisle.

"Let's go, Ms. Noel," Teddy said, gently holding Mary Jane by the elbow as she rose from her seat. He handed her on to Officer Daniels with instructions to take her to the station and process her hands and clothing. As soon as he turned back to her, Martha pounced on him.

"How dare you talk to Mary Jane like she's a common criminal!" she hissed. "You *know* she had nothing to do with Carla's murder. I don't know who did it, but Mary Jane was trying to *help* her, not *murder* her."

"Do you have proof of that? Were you there when Mary Jane supposedly discovered the body?"

"What do you mean, *supposedly*?"

He was silent.

"Well, no, I wasn't standing there when she discovered the body. But you are being ridiculous!"

"I'm doing my job," he said with a cold tone that made her see red.

"You're being a testosterone-driven moron is what you're doing."

"You may be needed for additional questioning tomorrow. Please don't leave town." She stared at him. He turned and walked out of the hall.

Martha flung herself into a chair, tears of anger and frustration popping from her eyes. As she sat there with her head in her hands, Allison Tomlinson and another Riley Creek police officer came in in full uniform. Allison's eyes and nose were puffy and she'd obviously been crying.

Martha stood. "Allison, what is it? Are you OK? Has something happened?"

"I just came in to let you know they've taken Mary Jane to the station. I don't want you to worry. They'll treat her fine. I'll find out what I can and talk to you tomorrow."

She's not as stiff as Teddy, but something is definitely off, Martha thought.

"But are *you* OK?" she asked again.

"I'll...I'll talk to you later," Allison said with a weak smile. "Right now, you all need to vacate the premises." Then she turned and walked out.

Margaret and Helen headed to the parking lot once the police had escorted them from the building and started stringing crime scene tape across the community center door. Martha retrieved Penny and joined them at the Subaru, and then she drove back toward the square, cursing most of the way. As soon as they got home, Penny, sensing Martha's mood, crawled into her lap as she phoned Albert. He'd been Aunt Lorna's faithful friend and attorney, and now Martha needed the attorney as much as she needed the friend.

"You've got to calm down and leave things alone for tonight," he said when she had told him what had happened. "The best thing you can do for Mary Jane is to take a hot bath, drink some tea, and get some sleep. We'll see what's happening in the morning. And if Mary Jane needs anything, though criminal law is not my area, I can help in a pinch."

Martha thanked him and wished him a good night, then set about following his advice.

Criminal law? This is insane!

She was too distracted to read a chapter of the new Olivia Blacke mystery that she'd been saving, which made her even more mad at Teddy. Somewhere between cursing at him and worrying about Mary Jane, she managed to drift off.

Martha and Penny were at the shop by six the next morning. PJ had beaten them to the punch, and coffee was already brewing. They'd hugged and consoled each other briefly, but agreed to get breakfast for the writers served and cleared away before talking about Mary Jane and the events of the night before. Since there were not yet any customers to check out, Penny headed straight upstairs to snuggle into her lambswool bed.

Martha thanked her lucky stars, not for the first time, that Riley Creekers had voted to make their village a dog-friendly community long before she and Penny had rolled into town. She remembered well the many times a forlorn Penny had had to stay behind or wait in the car when they'd lived in Boston.

As Martha filled the giant carafes for the self-service bar, she thought PJ's choices were perfect for the first full day of the retreat. She'd chosen Italian Roost (*dark, lots of body, and perfect for a jumpstart*), Sumatran Migration (*medium roast and always great to accompany a good book*), and Birder Blend (*light finish and just right for a morning hike*). Martha was happy she could pass her self-quiz on coffee types and features. At least *that* was one small item in the plus column today.

At around 6:30, Lew delivered armloads of fresh-baked breakfast items. Helen arrived while Martha was still arranging the croissants, bear claws and muffins onto the display pedestals inside the glass cases. PJ snapped a few pictures, checking them on her phone afterward to make sure she liked them. The first of the writers arrived at about 6:45, looking sleepy and anxious. Many had gotten visits from the police the night before, and were understandably jumpy and concerned about the turn of events.

Most took seats at tables near the back window, pointing at the various birds flying in and onto the giant platform feeder, and making feeble small talk. The cardinals, finches and wrens were especially active on this sunny morning, and Martha quietly thanked them for providing such distraction. She was glad to see that, so far, the bullying mockingbirds were focused on the special eating area she'd set up for them.

It's amazing what some mealworms and a couple handfuls of Craisins can do.

Martha and PJ moved table to table, reassuring the writers that the police were actively involved, that they had no reason to think the death was related to the retreat, and that they could continue their work and participate in the weekend's activities. Some looked dubious but, from their questions, they seemed to be trying to confirm they were safe rather than looking for reasons to leave.

By 7:00, the place was hopping with the writers who had signed up to attend Alexis's Sun Salutation Yoga on the square at 7:30. Martha spotted Alexis through the shop's front window. She was laying out mats of various colors and running an extension cord to a boom box. Within moments, the sound of Peruvian flutes wafted over and Alexis was stretching on a mat.

One by one, some of the writers began drifting out and onto the square. Others lingered behind, browsing the shop's shelves, a few whispering among themselves about Carla Innsbruck's murder. Martha saw one man with close-cropped black hair asking Helen about a pair of binoculars.

Please, please, please buy them. Thinking of how tight things would be this month, Martha had high hopes that there would be bird lovers among the group of nature writers who'd buy a souvenir or ten.

By 8:00, the writers had thinned out, no doubt to go commence their writing projects as the next guided event was not due to take place until early that afternoon. Sun Salutation Yoga was going strong, and Martha was relieved to see what looked to be at least ten beginners smiling and contorting on the square to Alexis's enthusiastic instruction.

Let's hope they stay this happy.

By 8:30, the yoga mats had been rolled up and the square cleared. Joanne and Margaret arrived and went next door, returning from Silent Sisters with Ethel Jean in tow. Dressed in a light flannel shirt, hiking pants and Hoka running shoes, Ethel Jean looked as if she had not slept a wink. Because she never wore make-up, the circles under her eyes were noticeably darker than usual.

The three took seats at a back table. PJ, who was busily tapping at a laptop on the counter, looked over to Martha and nodded, then pushed a few buttons on her phone and held it to her ear. Martha put together a plate of breakfast breads, a mint tea for Margaret, and coffees for Ethel Jean and Joanne. Lew came in and, after conferring with PJ briefly, took over the counter while PJ, Helen and Martha joined the other three at the table.

The click of tiny nails on hardwood sounded as Penny, roused from her beauty sleep, bounded across the shop floor and jumped into Ethel Jean's lap. Ethel Jean wrapped an arm around the terrier and pulled Penny into her chest. Martha gulped down the lump in her throat.

Joanne reached over to put her hand atop Ethel Jean's. For reasons only Joanne understood, she'd chosen orange for her day's ensemble.

"Move that hand or lose it, Orangina," Ethel Jean snarled.

So much for grief softening one's hard edges, Martha thought.

Pulling her hand away as if bitten by a snake, Joanne said, "Has anyone heard anything?"

Each one of the gang Martha referred to as "the gals" shared the little she knew. Ethel Jean had gone to the station and demanded to see Mary Jane. Teddy had told her that she was fine, but was being held in connection to "a recent crime" and Ethel Jean should go home. Mary Jane was to be interviewed today and there would be more information after that.

Martha shared that Albert had agreed to represent Mary Jane for the moment and she expected him to be with her for the morning's interview with the police. There wasn't much more to add, besides some clucking on Joanne's part and tears on Margaret's. Martha noticed none of them made mention of Teddy.

"This never would have happened without this friggin' retreat coming to town. We should shut the whole thing down," Ethel Jean said angrily, lifting her cup to her lips with a slightly trembling hand.

Martha was about to speak when PJ stepped in. "Now, Ethel Jean, I know you feel that way, but our friends and neighbors have invested too much time and money to do that. The best we can do is to put a brave face on things, and keep the writers busy so their minds stay off of the murder."

"Fine. Then Little Miss Sherlock Holmes here needs to find out who did it and get my sister out of jail. *Fast.*"

All eyes turned to Martha. "Why me?" she asked. "Teddy is working on it now and I'm sure he'll get to the bottom of it. We all just have to wait."

The group was quiet for a minute, and Martha caught Joanne, PJ, Helen and Margaret all exchange glances. Ethel Jean just glowered.

"What? Why are you all looking at each other like that?" Martha asked.

Helen cleared her throat. "Martha, heaven knows I'm far from perfect—you know that better than most—but Teddy...well, this is Teddy's first murder since being made chief and we think... that is to say..."

"Your boyfriend's gonna want to close this thing fast, whatever it takes. And right now he's looking at my sister as the fastest way to a case closed," Ethel Jean stated flatly.

Martha's mouth fell open. "That's not...you can't think he'd—"

"The man is driven. You may not be able to see that since you're thinking with your—"

PJ cut in. "What Ethel Jean means to say, honey, is that Teddy is going to have pressure on him to convict someone, and he may not know Mary Jane as well as the rest of us. You'd approach this murder from a different angle that he probably wouldn't be able to since your career isn't involved."

Martha took in their pleading eyes, which this time even included Ethel Jean's.

"OK, OK. The least I can do for Mary Jane is to poke around and see what I can find out. But this has to stay between us. Teddy will flip if he even *thinks* I'm getting involved."

PJ was the first to put her large manicured hand out into the middle of the table.

"For Mary Jane," she said, barely above a whisper.

One by one, the gals piled their hands on top of each other. Quietly, they all said, "For Mary Jane." Penny's paw, not quite long enough to reach, touched the edge of the table in agreement.

New Canaan, Tennessee, United States, Christmas week, 1890

THE NEWS OF THOMAS'S parents' death lay heavy on us all through the following weeks. The shorter days took my thoughts to home, and Mother and Cyril. Thomas put on a brave face, but I could tell his heart was not in our daily activities. Fortunately, the festivities of the season have brought us some lightness of heart.

While New Canaan citizens born in the United States are newer to the holiday, my German friends and English countrymen are most eager to share their traditions. We cut a large evergreen and placed it upright in a bucket in front of the mercantile shop. Children made strings of popcorn and nuts and wrapped them around the boughs. Seemingly from nowhere, the tree was covered in various types of ornamentation. There were glass baubles, intricately painted eggshells hanging from ribbons, and affixed to the top of the tree, a hand-cut tin star.

The preceding weeks had been busy, repairing outbuildings, harvesting corn and trapping, but seeing the tree one evening while walking back to my tent, I was struck by an almost physical pain thinking of my mother and brother so far away in England. Would I not have been better off at home, where I would be safely ensconced next to a fire that night, a glass of port in hand? I was still learning the farming and building arts. Could I really become self-sufficient and capable enough to support a family here on my own?

The melancholy I felt dissipated later that evening as the whole community gathered in our small church to sing songs, light candles, and celebrate the birth of our Savior. Later, we lit a fire by the stone *circle behind the mercantile and sang carols, roasted nuts, and shared stories of Christmases gone by. The Covingtons, a homestead family who'd lived a few miles outside the village since long before any of us had arrived, joined us and shared apples and honey produced from their own hives. Our wonderful Mr. Hicks gifted Thomas and me a new set of woodworking tools, and told us we represent the future of New Canaan. How proud we felt!*

However, we have recently begun to learn that New Canaan has two faces. One face is that of Christian charity and brotherhood, shown when the weather is fine and fortunes on the rise. The other face, pink-cheeked desperation and selfishness, emerged as the winter set in.

All summer, we enjoyed the best this land could offer. True enough, some days were so hot and the mosquitoes so thick, I questioned my own sanity and my decision to come here. Yet the community was happy. Trees were felled, crops were tended, and we all came together for church services, communal dinners, and even an occasional dance. These were happy times when I truly believed New Canaan was exactly what I'd wanted it to be: a new beginning for all.

Winters in England were somewhat mild, I have come to realize, made more so by the servants my brother employed to chop wood, clean fireplaces, and place warm water bottles between our cold sheets before bed. Here in Tennessee in 1890, I have no such creature comforts. The cold wind blows down, around and through these mountains and chills me thoroughly. Thomas and I thought surely one of our neighbors fortunate enough to have raised a roof already would offer to shelter us on the worst of nights. But we were mistaken. There is something about the dead of winter in a young community, something that causes it to retreat to its basest version of itself in order to survive. We men in the tents were offered the shelter of Mr. Hicks's paddock, and thanks to that escaped frostbite, but our fellow New Canaanites shuttered themselves and their homes to focus what little resources they had on their immediate families.

What felt like abundance in the summer has transformed into measured bites that will have to last many mouths to the first thaw. Thomas and I are largely on our own. We trudge through the valley all night, breaking up the ice in the water troughs for farmers who pay us a pittance. We return to the paddock to warm up, sleep a bit, then the cycle repeats itself, night after night, week after week. We are short with one another due to lack of sleep and so little food.

When Mrs. Jesperson was found frozen to death in her small cabin, it was Thomas and I who were asked to carry her frail body to a storage barn until the ground thawed enough for her burial. We did the task to earn a few pennies, but never spoke of it aloud to one another. The pennies equal food and food means warmth in our bellies.

We see that food, shelter, and warmth are all our neighbors can focus on, and we have come to a similar understanding ourselves. These moments of desperation and hunger are what my mother had feared for me, and I will never tell her, in person or in letter, how miserably these weeks have passed. Even now, my fingers can barely grasp the pencil and I warm them against the glass of the lamp to scratch out one more sentence.

We are balancing on the edge of a knife some nights now. Thomas and I are resolved to earn as much as possible in the spring, surviving on as little as we can, so that by next winter we will have a roof above us and a floor beneath us.

Chapter Six

The gals dispersed. The others in the group had managed to convince Ethel Jean to go back home to rest for a few hours, and Lew agreed to cover Silent Sisters. He'd seemed happy to do so, raising his laptop in the air and explaining that he had a final paper to write and the quiet time would be helpful. Martha knew he was a senior at nearby Lewis High and planning to attend college on an academic scholarship in the fall. He'd be sorely missed by the gals who'd watched him grow and mature into a young man.

Helen and PJ resumed work in the shop, where a few writers and birders were drinking coffee and browsing. Margaret headed off to help set up the afternoon's retreat activities and Joanne had an appointment at Looking Sharp. Following a running Penny up the stairs, Martha wondered how she'd gotten herself involved in yet another murder investigation.

At least I didn't find the body this time. She quickly dismissed the thought as she contemplated Mary Jane sitting in a jail cell. *First things first. I've got to figure out who Carla Innsbruck is. Was.*

Martha fired up her computer and clicked on Google, again thinking how nice it was to finally have a solid internet connection. She resisted checking her website for orders or the shop email account for messages, trusting Helen and PJ to monitor them.

Will social media really do anything to boost our sales? she wondered absently. *This whole online thing is probably a waste of time.*

Don't most people just head to their local Piggly Wiggly, Kroger or Whole Foods to get their coffee?

Returning her attention to the search bar, Martha plugged in Carla Innsbruck's name. She needed to know more about this mystery woman.

She found a short Wikipedia entry, noting her specifics. *Born in 1956 in Orono, Maine, to parents David and Cathy. Attended University of California at Berkeley, active in disability rights, shifted focus to the environment shortly after marrying Brian Nelson, another Berkeley grad. Nelson had gone on to get his PhD, became an ornithologist, and now occupied an endowed professorship at one of the campuses in the North Carolina system. And—small world indeed—from his page on the university's website, it looked like he had some connection to the future Moreno Center for World Bird Conservation.*

Ana must know him!

Brian and Carla had had no children and had broken up sometime in the nineties, but during the time of their marriage, she had authored several seminal works about industry's harmful impacts on the environment. One had become a bestseller. Martha clicked on a few more sites to check out Carla's books and recognized some of the covers she'd seen in the crowd at the keynote the evening before.

Carla and a few others had broken into a federal land management office in 2006 and splashed pigs' blood all over the computers to protest deforestation, which she argued led to the extinction of several species of birds and mammals. She was arrested and, as ringleader, spent ten years in the Virginia Correctional Center for Women. She was released in 2017 and had spent the past five years living outside of Riverton and penning various op-ed pieces for small environmental publications.

Martha thought about what she'd read and clicked on some reviews of Carla's books. Had the woman still been living off of these royalties?

So, how does a woman who gave up ten years of her life over deforestation suddenly decide the best way to protect the environment is to hasten the destruction of the planet?

She decided she needed to talk to the one person that knew the pre-prison Carla Innsbruck: Brian Nelson. She'd just written an email to Ana Moreno, asking her if she could make the introduction, when she heard someone tromping up the stairs. From the heavy footfalls, she guessed it to be PJ. Instead, in walked Allison in full police uniform, the heavy steps caused by her sturdy black boots. She looked a bit better than the last time Martha had seen her, but not much.

Martha stood, but sat back down once Allison took a seat on the daybed against the wall on the other side of the room.

"How's Mary Jane?" Martha asked without preamble.

"I haven't been able to talk to her, but from what I've heard, she's holding up. All the officers at RCPD know her so she's being as well cared for as can be managed under the circumstances. When I left the station, Teddy was going to begin interviewing her. Albert is with her."

"OK," said Martha. "But I still say this is ridiculous. Mary Jane Noel was a nurse, for crying out loud. She wouldn't hurt a fly."

"I know. I believe you, but the evidence isn't pretty. She was found bending over the body, her hands covered in blood, and by her own admission, her watch was in the victim's hand."

"I know, I know. Don't remind me," Martha said miserably. "By the by, what was going on with you yesterday? You looked really upset. Was it about Mary Jane being arrested?"

"Well yes, but also no," Allison said, tears welling up. Martha was quiet, knowing that often silence worked better than any other prompt. "You know how I told you once that I worked for the FBI back in Nashville before I came to Riley Creek?"

"Yes." Martha recalled Allison giving her a very abridged bio back in the fall.

"Well, one thing I didn't go into was the relationship I was in. It's a really long story which I don't think I can tell right now without totally losing it, but I lived with a woman named Callie and her son Noah. He was only one year old when we met. She'd left his dad recently."

Seeing Martha raise her eyebrows, Allison said with a sad laugh, "Callie always said she wasn't gay or straight. She fell in love with spirits, not bodies.

"Anyway, back then—it was about 2010 until 2016—I thought she was 'the one' and that the three of us were going to be a family forever. Maybe we'd even welcome another kid or two," she said, the tears now flowing freely down her face. "That never happened, obviously. I was totally absorbed in work and all I could think of was moving up the ranks. I got involved in a case where we broke up a human trafficking ring. I don't think I was even home for the last two weeks of that one.

"Fast forward to the end where she told me that she wanted a relationship with *me*, not with an empty chair at the dinner table. I guess she decided that growing up with a single parent was as good for Noah as growing up with two parents, one of whom was never home. And so, one day, I came home to an empty house.

"I was absolutely devastated, but she left no forwarding information. Once the case wrapped up, I hit the wall, and shortly after left the FBI and came to Riley Creek to get myself back together and create a different kind of life. Sure, I'd become successful, but it cost me everything. *Every*thing."

By now, Martha had supplied Allison with a tissue box that read "Blow Me" on the outside. Allison wiped at her eyes and nose.

"Yesterday, I got a call from a public attorney in Memphis, where I guess she and Noah have been living. Callie died last week. Cancer. The attorney says she has no next of kin and that she left my name and number with the hospice center. Noah is staying with a neighbor at their apartment complex."

Martha went to sit next to Allison and put an arm around her shoulder, which required more effort than she'd expected thanks to the bulletproof vest under Allison's uniform shirt and the radio handset clipped to her shoulder.

"What are you going to do?" she asked.

"I have no clue, but I have to do *something*," Allison replied. "Noah must be twelve or thirteen now, his mother just died, and it sounds like he's all alone. I don't think Teddy will like it, especially during a murder investigation, but I've gotta get to Memphis. I'm sorry I can't stay to help Mary Jane, but Noah needs my help just as much. Joanne already agreed to ride with me, to help keep me awake for the long drive and for moral support."

She stood up and shook her head as if to clear it, then snapped her fingers. "Oh, before I forget. We're trying to find out about Carla Innsbruck's manager. Mary Jane says she's named Sherry? Can you or Ethel Jean find her address? No one is answering the phone number Mary Jane used to contact her."

Martha double-checked her inbox to see if Ana had written back. Seeing that she hadn't, she headed down the stairs with Penny close at her heels. She asked PJ to ask Ethel Jean if she could find an address for Sherry and checked her watch. It was time for the first author check-in at Toad in a Hole.

"Come on, gal. Time to meet with our nature-loving scribes." Penny smiled up and trotted along at Martha's feet.

Joanne exited Looking Sharp across the square as Martha and Penny came out the front door of Birds 'n' Beans, and she motioned Martha over. Martha wasn't sure what to say about Joanne's magenta-hued hair, but she didn't have to wait long.

Patting her hair with one hand, Joanne said, "*Très bien*, no? I'm going on a road trip with Allison, but I hope to be back for the retreat's closing ceremony."

Martha said, "Yes, I heard." Nodding at Joanne's new do, she added, "Very striking indeed."

"Look at this," Joanne said, pulling her phone out of her purse and scrolling through apps. She tapped and scrolled again quickly, then held the phone up to Martha's face. "Look!"

Martha skimmed the text on the screen, surmising the piece was an op-ed from a nearby town newspaper. The author, Liz Waterson, reminisced about the "old Carla Innsbruck," mentioned a few horrible details from the keynote speech of the evening before, and without saying it outright, implied that someone who advocated for the end of the human race ought not to be missed too darn much. The op-ed was an ugly piece, but did a credible job of likening Carla's keynote to hate speech.

"Liz is one of our writers!" Martha exclaimed. "At the retreat. In fact, she was one of a small group who stayed around last night after Mary Jane said she was locking up the church. I saw her out on the square at yoga this morning."

"But she's practically *making* herself a suspect with this piece, isn't she?" Joanne asked.

Could this murder enter the Guinness Book of Records *for quickest mystery solved?* Martha mused. *One of the people close by Carla at the time of her death just happens to advertise in the newspaper the next day that she found Carla pretty distasteful.*

"Talk about terrible timing," she said to Joanne, and puffed out a breath that filled her cheek. She wished Joanne a safe trip with Allison, then they parted and Martha headed to Toad in a Hole for the writers' noon check-in. Upon arrival, she did a quick headcount and saw that all of the eighteen writers were present. There seemed to be a buzz that had been absent at breakfast.

Octavius quickly pulled Martha aside. "You're our President of the R-C," he said urgently, wringing his hands. "You've got to talk to them or I'm afraid they'll all want to leave and get their money back."

Martha nodded, and then stepped forward, looking around at the chatty group and trying to get their attention. Suddenly, an ear-splitting whistle sounded. Snapping her head around, Martha took in Margaret removing her index finger and thumb from her mouth and reddening from the attention. She nodded to Martha to begin.

"Friends, as you know, I'm Martha Sloane, President of the Retailers' Collective here in Riley Creek. I know you've heard of the unfortunate circumstances surrounding last night's keynote speaker—"

"Good riddance," came a voice from the assembled group, though Martha hadn't caught the source of the statement.

"—but I want to assure you, our law enforcement partners are on the case and expect to have the killer in custody shortly. In the meantime, our goal is to provide you with a beautiful home away from home where you can work on your writing project and network with other nature writers."

"But will we *really* be safe?" asked one older man, a bit tentatively. "The police came to all of our cabins after breakfast this morning and said we aren't to leave town, and that they may want to interview us. We only signed up for a weekend event, not an extended stay."

Martha nodded patiently, trying to convey that everything was fine, just fine. "There were a small group of you that stayed around after the logistics meeting last night. The police will likely want to talk to those individuals just to see if they may have noticed any important details."

She couldn't help but meet Liz Waterson's eye as she spoke. The woman sat, chin up and shoulders back.

"Or maybe to see if they might have killed Carla Innsbruck? And then written an article about it?" Nick the photographer asked and smirked, turning his head slightly in Liz's direction. He slumped back casually, wrists covered in leather bracelets and one arm kicked back atop his chair.

What an alpha, Martha thought.

"I think it's best if you all go on about your business. As of now, Chief Perry hasn't told us anything about a safety concern that would cause us to end the retreat early. Please carry on as normal, and we'll see you at the Intro to Birding workshop, behind Toad in a Hole down by the river."

She stepped back to make it clear that she'd completed her remarks. Octavius and Margaret circulated among the group, forced smiles plastered on, trying to make small talk.

The show must go on.

Martha left the bookshop once the writers seemed to have settled and was heading across the square when PJ intercepted her.

"Honey, Ana wrote you back. Also, I popped over to Ethel Jean's. We went into Mary Jane's side of the duplex and looked everywhere for information about Carla's manager. We couldn't find a scrap of info, but you know Mary Jane. Ever since we started getting a better signal, she's taken to keeping everything in her phone."

Martha contemplated how to find someone's address if you didn't know their number. Yellow pages? Negative. Internet? Nope. An ad in the paper? Not likely. Then she remembered Mary Jane mentioning the contractor who'd served as her initial connection to Carla Innsbruck. At least that was a place to start.

New Canaan, Tennessee, United States, February 1, 1891

THOMAS AND I HAD NO idea when Susannah would arrive, but never in the time we had to expect her did we think it would be so soon after her letter.

She arrived just weeks after Christmas.

The weather following the holiday was erratic, one day snowy and the next as fair as a gentle spring day. The day Susannah arrived, the sun had made it warm enough to carry out the next phase of construction and a group of the men were working on the post office. I was atop the roof, pounding in shingles while others were working on the porch, when I saw the postal carrier in his distinctive brown wagon a distance away, but thought nothing of it. It was only when I heard Thomas exclaim that I looked down to see a female form alighting from the wagon. Thomas ran to her and the two embraced; here was Susannah.

Coming down from my perch to meet her, I saw immediately that she shared Thomas's keen green eyes and dimples, but where he had dark wavy hair, hers was bright yellow. Though she was Thomas's sister, I could not help but note her flattering figure. She'd taken the train from Boston to Raleigh, then various coaches all the way to Knoxville, and then on to New Canaan. She was exhausted from the long journey, and she and Thomas were understandably emotional as they recounted the tragic loss of their parents.

As Thomas took her off to his tent to rest, I returned to my work. That afternoon, Thomas made arrangements with the Petersons, a young family with a spare room in their modest farmhouse. They would allow Susannah to stay in their room in exchange for Thomas *helping Mr. Peterson butcher a winter pig. That night, she settled at the inn, our tents being no place for a young lady and certainly not for one so in need of rest and recovery.*

As for Thomas and me, again we settled that night in Mr. Hicks's barn with pillows and blankets, happy for the bit of warmth put out by the wood stove. Our tents were still welcome accommodations on those evenings when the temperatures were mild, but that bitter night we rested toe to toe. With Susannah's arrival, we recalculated our building plans and decided that we would begin the first of our two houses as soon as the weather allowed.

That night, I told Thomas of the extra bit of money from my brother that I had placed in the bank. I told him that he was welcome to what part of it he needed to supplement his own nest egg and get a home built for him and his sister. After all, she could not reside indefinitely with the Petersons. We slept that night in a spirit of bonhomie, sure that only good lay in store for all of us.

Chapter Seven

Martha and Penny followed PJ back to the store. They headed right up to the office where Martha checked her email. Ana had indeed responded, sending along Brian Nelson's contact info.

Martha tapped the number into her phone. Nelson picked up on the second ring, and waited while Martha explained how she'd come by his number. She offered her condolences, apologized for disturbing him, and explained that she was trying to gather a bit of background on Carla.

"Let me get this straight. You were with Carla when she was murdered?" he asked. Martha couldn't assess his emotional state yet, but was prepared for several possible reactions. This *was* his murdered ex-wife they were talking about, after all.

Martha explained that she had been in the same building, but not actually with Carla when she died. She expressed her condolences again.

"Save your breath," Nelson said gruffly. "I'd thought about murdering that woman about a hundred times myself. Looks like someone just beat me to it."

Martha stood with the phone to her ear and mouth hanging open, unsure how to respond. *OK, that was NOT one of the reactions I'd anticipated.*

"Look," he said, "you've gotta understand, we were great for a few years. Eventually, I went mainstream to pay the bills, but Carla never stopped heading to the nearest political action. She just became more sophisticated, doing her protesting through speeches and books.

"Things fell apart once I had to start the dog and pony show of earning tenure. She just couldn't understand me needing to do research on songbirds hitting buildings instead of picketing a housing development. We drifted apart."

"Songbirds hitting buildings?" Martha asked. He'd lost her there.

"Yep. My research centers on why particular species of birds—for example, certain warbler species—hit glass buildings while they are on migratory night flights at a higher rate than other species. It's been a significant problem, especially given the general decline of bird species in the U.S. Now my work focuses more on consulting with cities and municipalities to help them reduce the numbers of bird strikes occurring around their larger buildings."

Martha was fascinated. She'd never even thought about this. Had migrating birds hit some of the large buildings on the campus where she'd worked in Boston?

"But what can cities really do? Don't birds just... do what they do?"

Nelson gave a friendly laugh. "There's a long answer, but in a nutshell, there are lots of things that can be done, many very inexpensively. Simply turning out the internal lights in buildings at night reduces the chances of attracting migrating birds."

"That's amazing. I've never thought about birds migrating at night and flying into buildings, to be honest."

"Don't worry, you're not alone. But back to Carla... you won't believe this, but we never even bothered to get divorced. For a long time, it just wasn't important. She led her life, I led mine. But when I met Ashley, my partner, back in 2000, I asked for a divorce and

Carla refused. Ashley and I moved in together and here I was, still married to another woman. To be honest, I nearly lost Ashley over the whole thing.

"It wasn't until she went to prison back in 2007 that I finally petitioned the court and a judge granted the divorce. I'm angry now just thinking about what she put me through, and Ashley by extension. I'm not really glad someone killed her, but she does have a way of bringing out strong feelings in people."

"Well, she certainly did so last night when she gave her keynote," Martha said, then gave Nelson a brief description of Carla's *Let the Earth Go* remarks. He was incredulous.

"Are you kidding? I hadn't talked to Carla in years, but that sounds far out, especially for a dyed-in-the-wool environmentalist. Do you think something happened to her? Like was she drunk or something?"

"I have no idea, but she didn't seem like she was. To be honest, I never really spoke to her, except for introducing her at the start of her talk and thanking her at the end. And by the way, would you happen to know her agent, Sherry?" Martha figured she had nothing to lose by asking.

"Nope. I have no connection to her friends or associates."

"Well, thanks anyway," Martha replied. "You've been very generous with your time."

"Will you... let me know if you find out what happened? Just for old times' sake, you know?" Nelson asked.

"Definitely," Martha replied, then added, "And would you do me a favor? I'm looking into this pretty unofficially, so if anyone from the police calls you, do you mind keeping this conversation between us?"

"Absolutely. And Martha? One more thing. Ana said you are going to be supplying the center with coffee for the coffee shop. Your beans *are* bird-friendly, right?"

Martha assured him her beans were very bird-friendly, and then they ended the call.

"Bird-friendly *beans*?" she asked Penny. The terrier looked back at her and cocked her head, clearly in Martha's camp on this one. Martha made a note to ask Helen what in the world Nelson was talking about.

Martha and Penny took the stairs down and whisked out of the shop. Martha's head was spinning with all that Nelson had shared. He'd actually said *he'd* thought about murdering Carla. Was that proof that he should be considered a suspect or proof of just the opposite? The man had a PhD. Wasn't he smart enough to avoid incriminating himself?

The spring air hit Martha and she realized she'd been so absorbed in retreat preparation, the tragic events of Thursday night and Mary Jane's subsequent arrest that she hadn't done a run or taken a hike in days. Looking down at Penny, she laughed as the dog's beard ruffled in the wind and she lifted her nose to the breeze to catch the day's happenings.

"Silly," Martha said. "We've gotta get up in the mountains as soon as this is over. We promised we were going to do better about having balance, right?"

Penny let out a juicy sneeze as a strong wind wafted up her open nostrils.

"Bless you," Martha said and shook her head. "Come on." They took the sidewalk over to where Jimmy was on a ladder at one of the hanging baskets and Delores was handing the hose up to him.

"Beautiful! Those look so great. Is it not too much work for you two to water them?" Martha asked. The Ritzenwallers were energetic, she knew, but still were "of an age," as Aunt Lorna would have put it.

"We're just fine," said Delores while Jimmy watered. "Lew is watering the standing pots every other day and we do these hanging baskets and the pots at the community center once a week. This time of year, that's enough water for them. And we enjoy it."

Jimmy handed the hose down to Delores and stepped down from the ladder. "How are things?" he asked Martha. Delores headed to the spigot on the wall to turn off the water, then began picking a few dead leaves from one of the nearby potted arrangements.

"Fine, so far. The writers understandably had lots of questions today, but I think we managed to reassure them that they are safe and there is no reason to cancel the retreat. So far, that is," she added in a worried tone.

"I take it you are looking into this... matter?" Jimmy asked with an eyebrow raised.

"Yes, I'm doing a little... background research, you might say," Martha said, giving him a wink.

He nodded his head and asked if Chief Perry was aware of her research.

"*Wellll...*" she trailed off. "Not just yet."

"I see," he said. "This is where I make a desperate appeal to you to please be careful, and I remind you that there may be a killer somewhere in the village, if he or she hasn't already hightailed it out of here."

"Message received. Hey, have either of you seen Frank? I need to talk to him about something related to my research."

"Somehow, he's managing to work in the hardware store," Delores said, rejoining them. "We visited with him for a few minutes, only long enough to tell that he's barely slept and is terribly worried about Mary Jane. He knows he can't do much at the moment except make sure she's got solid legal representation. He said he went to the police station last night and again this morning, and they still won't let him see her."

Martha reassured the Ritzenwallers that she would check on Frank while she was in Elder's Hardware. They talked her into letting Penny stay with them so she could enjoy the outdoors a bit more.

Martha made a beeline through the stand of oak trees, spring leaves shimmering a translucent green, and entered Frank's hardware store. He was behind the register bagging up some paint rollers for a man dressed in a painters' cap, dirty white t-shirt and white pants stained with every paint color in the rainbow. As Frank bid the man a "See ya next time, Hank," Martha made sure there were no other customers nearby, and then approached him.

"Frank, how can you work today?" she asked in a whisper, taking in his exhausted face. Had he not even shaved?

"I can't just stay up in my apartment, Martha," Frank replied. "I'll go bonkers. Albert is calling me later, after the interviews this morning. No offense, but your boyfriend has lost his damn mind thinking Mary Jane had anything to do with that woman's death." Tears shimmered along the edges of his eyes.

Martha knew she had to tread carefully. She didn't want to say anything bad about Teddy, but she could tell Frank was in no mood for disagreement.

"It's a terrible situation, Frank, and I'm doing all I can to see if there's more I can find out. Can you tell me anything about how

Mary Jane got connected to Carla Innsbruck? She said something to me about a contractor who'd come in here to your shop."

Frank let out a coarse groan. "Bah, I wish I'd never said a word. One of my regulars, Scott, said something to me about working on some famous lady's roof. He told me it was Innsbruck and I was dumb enough to mention it to Mary Jane. Next thing I know, she's asking Scott to make the introduction."

He shook his head and rubbed a callous on the pad of one large hand. "As I recall it, she never actually met Innsbruck. Scott gave her the woman's number and Mary Jane called it, but as soon as she told the Innsbruck woman why she was calling, the old bat gave her the number for some other woman at her publishing company, told her to call her, and hung up the phone."

Her publishing company? Martha thought. *That's a bit different. I thought Mary Jane said she'd only dealt with her agent. Is that the same thing? Is this an inconsistency, the kind that detectives Gemma James and Duncan Kincaid always warn about in Deborah Crombie's mysteries?*

"Is there a way I could talk to your contractor friend? The one that worked on Carla's roof?" Martha asked.

"Sure. I'll find out his schedule for tomorrow and call you as soon as I have it. And hey—by the way—I'm due down at the police station tomorrow to explain this whole Innsbruck connection to Chief Perry."

"I see. Perhaps until then, the fact that I've asked you anything about it could stay between us?" Martha asked lightly.

"You know it. Please help get Mary Jane out of this, Martha. You know she didn't do it," Frank implored.

"I'm doing my darnedest, Frank. Promise."

The activity scheduled for the writers that early evening was Intro to Birding with Don. He'd planned to bring enough sets of binoculars to the riverbank behind Toad in a Hole for anyone interested to get a primer on how to use them to identify some area birds.

Martha had finished out the afternoon at the shop, then walked Penny to the Ritzenwallers to hang out with Fritz while she helped at the evening workshop. Penny, unsurprisingly, was thoroughly displeased with this turn of events, not in the least bit interested in Martha's explanation about dogs not being conducive to the attraction of birds. She barely wagged a tail in Martha's direction when she headed back toward the square.

Martha was pleased when she arrived at the grassy slope behind Toad in a Hole to see that about ten of the writers had shown up for the workshop. She waved up to a smiling Octavius who was standing in the sail-shaped window in the back of the store. He jerked a thumb over his shoulder, and then made typing motions. She nodded and gave him a thumbs-up. The others were writing. This was good. That was what they'd come here to do.

Don welcomed the group and shared a bit about the history of birdwatching. Martha was always surprised when he reminded her that the study of birds went back as far as the mid-1800s in Victorian England, and that the Audubon Society was founded in the U.S. in 1905. She had thought of birding as a more contemporary pastime, but as Don told the group, it had a long history that began with a wish to protect birds from the feather trade.

Once Don concluded his brief history lesson, the group got down to business. Fortunately for those gathered, a circle of rough grey boulders peeking up through the grass turned the area into a natural classroom. He passed out sets of binoculars to each person, encouraging them to put the strap around their neck. He then explained how to adjust them to fit properly. Martha smiled, recalling that Aunt Lorna had always called this "tuning her binocs." Don led the group through adjusting the fit to the eyes so that two fields of view became one, positioning the eye cups appropriately for those wearing glasses and those without, and setting the focus.

Martha overheard several of the group exclaim that they'd never really done this with binoculars before; that they'd simply put them up to their eyes and looked through. Don overheard this too.

"This will put a whole new lease on your optic life," he told the group. He then explained that dawn and dusk were the more active times of day for birds and encouraged the group to simply look around the area using their binoculars, seeing if they could spot any movement in the trees or shrubs. The writers stood up and wandered around, looking a little bit, Martha thought, like a gathering of ornithological zombies who'd wandered off the set of *The Walking Dead*.

When one writer spotted a bird, the whole group turned and aimed their binoculars at the same spot. Don used each new sighting to teach them how to sharpen their field of view by using just the center wheel on the binoculars. Martha joined in, quickly adjusting a spare set of binoculars and looking around the rushing river for movement.

The group spotted brilliant red cardinals, blue jays, mourning doves, Eastern bluebirds, and a turkey vulture soaring overhead. Martha reminded herself again that she really needed to take a hike one of these days, especially with the spring migrating birds coming through soon.

"Wow! I see these birds every day, but never stopped to really watch them. Do you sell binoculars anywhere around here? How about bird books?" Martha couldn't decide which made her happier: the joy of a new birder or the suggestion of future sales.

"Look at that one! I think I see white stripes on its wings," one writer said excitedly. Martha recalled her name was Sally and that she was a bartender from the Nashville area. Sally pointed up into a stand of trees across the water with one hand, the other still holding the binoculars to her eyes.

The group easily caught sight of the bird Sally was watching, because there was a pair of them, jerkily chasing each other in and out of a thicket of mountain laurel. Martha's eyes confirmed what she'd expected to see: two brownish grey mockingbirds, each a bit larger than a robin, with pale creamy breasts and bright white wingbars flashing as they darted after each other, chirping at one another.

"Nice birds!" Don said. "You've got two northern mockingbirds there. They're likely courting and getting ready to nest. They'll squawk at you and really carry on if you get too close."

"That's kind of silly," Sally said. "Doing that just draws more attention, doesn't it?"

"I guess that's right, now that you mention it," Don said, laughing.

"Do they really sing other birds' songs?" another writer asked.

"Yes, they sure do," Don replied. "In fact, they've been known to learn over one hundred songs throughout their lives, as well as other random sounds from their environments. Scientists aren't sure why, though they think it has to do with attracting mates or telling other birds to stay away from their nests."

"But doesn't squawking at other birds like that also call attention to the fact that there may be a nest nearby?"

"True, and that's a good point. I guess the mystery of bird logic is part of what makes them so fascinating. If you'd like to learn more about them, I know Mr. Bennett has an excellent selection of bird books up at the shop."

The workshop came to a close and Martha helped Don collect the binoculars and store them in a Tupperware bin in the back of his truck. Several of the writers broke off to go to Toad in a Hole in search of bird books for sale.

"Great job, Don. And thank you, mockingbirds!" Martha made a swooping gesture in the direction of the bushes where the two lovers had been spotted.

"What's not to love about birds that impersonate other birds? Mother Nature never ceases to amaze."

Indeed, thought Martha. *Indeed.*

Bringing herself back to the moment, she turned to Don and asked, "Hey, by the way, have you seen Liz Waterson? She's one of our writers for the weekend and I was hoping to talk to her about the article she wrote for the paper about Carla Innsbruck. Is she staying up at the cabins?"

Don shook his head. "Nope. Since she's local, I think she decided to spend evenings at home. She's staying at that new house she's building out on Rhubarb Pike. You might try there if you're looking for her."

Rhubarb Pike. That made Martha think of Donna Riggs and the first time she'd encountered a dead body last year. Martha smiled to think of Donna, survivor of hard times and now her friend.

Our retreat may be a disaster, we may have another dead body on our hands, but as Aunt Lorna would have said, I've gotta keep on keepin' on.

New Canaan, Tennessee, United States, April 20, 1891

IT HAS BEEN SOME TIME since I could sit quietly and write in these pages, for so much has happened.

Susannah and Thomas and I spent the last months of winter planning for their home. Let me change that: OUR home. After much discussion, Thomas and I decided that, because I was putting forward a significant investment for the house we would build, it would be owned jointly. We are making a kind of "duplicate" house, in which one side mirrors the other. I will live in one side, and Thomas and Susannah in the other. I suspect that we will eventually build a second home and have separate households, but for now I remain full of energy and enthusiasm, driven by the thought of living not in a tent and not in a barn, but finally beneath a roof and between solid walls once again.

In February and March, when our work was not stopped by heavy snowfall or the need to hold an impromptu snowball war, we borrowed the Petersons' horse and steer team to clear the land we'd bought from Mr. Hicks. It is lovely; a bit outside the hub of town, but close enough to hear the church bells. Thomas and I plan to orient the house so that the morning sun hits the front porch.

The front of the house is also where Susannah wishes to have her garden. Many of our compatriots clear every tree from their land as they prepare to build, but we are partial to the large oaks that are so common here, and so have left two of them, one towering on either side of the house. Really, Thomas and I share the same views on so many things, and I constantly thank my good fortune to have crossed his path so soon after arriving in New Canaan.

Susannah continues to live with the Petersons and they seem to get on well. Some days, she helps in the kitchen at the inn, and on others she assists Mrs. Peterson with their children or other tasks at the farm. When she is free and the weather is pleasant, she brings a blanket and a packed lunch and she, Thomas and I sit on our land and dream about what we will be doing at our house once it is built. Bluebirds and wrens flit in and out of the flowering redbud trees that dot the forest edges. They are as grateful for spring as are we.

We each have a unique daydream and we can recite each other's almost by heart now. I dream of inviting Mother and Cyril to New Canaan and playing tennis on the lawn with Thomas, Cyril and Susannah. Thomas dreams of a shooting club that meets at our house for brandy on the porch after a successful hunt. Susannah's tastes run less to sport and more to the dramatic, for she daydreams about theatrical productions acted out on the second floor porch.

The rector from our New Canaan church, who is also the town schoolmaster, came by to visit us one day as we sat daydreaming. He asked us the name of our future household, and we have been bordering on obsession with the question since it was posed. Some homes in New Canaan are named after the family who constructed them, examples being the Peterson Farm and the Galion House. Others are named after naturally occurring phenomena near the home, such as Tall Maples and Five Stones. We continue to ponder this question, experimenting with variations on Riley and Hoffmann, but we have come to no conclusions as of yet.

I will close by sharing one more bit of exciting news. The weather has allowed us to make ample progress on the library's construction and Mr. Hicks recently asked Susannah if she would become its care-

taker when it opens later this year. She has said yes and now we look forward to a somewhat steady, if modest, course of income to add to our coffers. May our good fortune never end.

Chapter Eight

Martha woke up bright and early, thanks to Penny who'd jumped down from the bed and was pacing back and forth, her tiny nails tapping along the bedroom's wide oak planks.

"OK, OK," Martha grumbled, slipping feet into slippers and heading downstairs. She opened the French doors to let Penny out to collect canine news updates, then set to brewing some Sumatran Migration.

"I know you're supposed to be good for reading or ruminating," she said to the scoops of coffee as she measured them into her French press. "And I need both today."

She let Penny back in just as the kettle sounded. A few more minutes and she depressed the plunger on the press and poured the dark goodness into Aunt Lorna's "Easily Distracted by Birds" mug, along with a splash of cream. Trundling back up the stairs with Penny alongside, she settled her steaming mug onto a quilted coaster, got back in bed, and pulled the covers up. Penny vaulted onto the bed and curled up in a circle against her hip. She reached for the Olivia Blacke mystery she'd been saving for weeks and opened it to the first page.

Cracking the fresh spine, Martha thought of Mary Jane and her voracious appetite for books. *Does she have anything to read in the prison cell? Surely Albert or Frank have taken her something to help pass the time? And surely she will be allowed to leave Riley Creek Police Department today?* Martha sipped her coffee, the open book remaining unread. How could she stay here, comfy in bed with a freshly opened cozy mystery, while one of her closest friends remained alone and possibly bookless in a prison cell, all because of an idea Martha herself had cooked up as leader of the Retailers' Collective?

Nope. Not happening.

She threw back the covers and jumped out of bed, leaving her steaming "Easily Distracted" mug atop the unread mystery.

Don had mentioned Liz spent nights at the house she was building out on Rhubarb Pike. As Martha pulled her Subaru station wagon out onto the road, she thought of Donna Riggs and the first time she'd gone out to her trailer there in search of answers about her murdered grandson, Curtis.

That seems like a lifetime ago, Martha thought. *And here I go again.*

In a few minutes, she was cruising along the rural road, passing the Kubota farm machinery outpost and the ancient Chevron gas station she recalled from her trip last fall. Penny had promptly fallen back to sleep in the passenger seat. Wondering how she'd recognize Liz Waterson's house, Martha had just thought about stopping to call Don when she spotted a Bobcat and a trench digger parked in a field that looked to have been recently cleared of trees. A freshly dug trench that ran along the road held brand new PVC piping. Perpendicular to this trench ran another leading alongside a muddy drive to a large new home set back from the road. Martha was relieved to see that, though trees had been cleared to make way for the sewer, water lines, driveway, and yard, a large stand of pine behind the home had been untouched.

She was no expert, but she had to admit it was a stunning home. Two stories, its modern architecture held elements of the

Arts and Crafts movement Aunt Lorna had loved so much: a large covered porch, wood trim, mullioned windows, and dark grey river rock that made the house look as if it had sprung from the land around it. A three-car garage was connected to the house and featured many of the same design elements, with the exception that it was still wrapped in white plastic sporting the word "TYVEK."

Martha briefly explained to Penny that dogs weren't always welcome in brand new homes and got a stink eye in return. She took a bracing sip from her to-go coffee mug, closed the car door and headed for the house. The retreat events didn't start until later today, so would Liz be awake? It was 8:30 in the morning, but not everyone was an early bird, Martha knew.

She knocked on the heavy walnut door, trying to see through the grid of glass panels that decorated its top third. She was just contemplating how much Aunt Lorna would have loved the exposed beams that lined the porch's ceiling when she heard the sound of a lock being opened and the door swung wide.

Liz Waterson was up and fully dressed, sporting burgundy leather clogs, tan khaki pants, and a quarter zip fleece top decorated with tiny tents and campfires. Her hair was in a ponytail that threaded through the hole in the back of her Boston Red Sox cap. Martha had noticed Liz's pear shape at the community center a couple nights ago, and now, close up, pegged her at about five feet tall.

"Nice clogs," Liz said neutrally, pointing down at Martha's feet. If not for the fact that they were olive green, they were a perfect match for Liz's dark red pair.

"Thanks," Martha replied, a bit disarmed as she'd anticipated a frosty reception.

"Come on in," Liz said. "Coffee? I just made some. It's bird-friendly, so I think you'll like it."

What is with the bird-friendly coffee? I've got to remember to ask Helen about that.

"Yes. Sure. Thanks," Martha said, hearing her own voice and thinking she sounded like a prize idiot.

"Guess you must be a morning person, owning a coffee shop and all?" Liz said over her shoulder as they entered the most gorgeous kitchen Martha had ever seen. It was the epitome of a farmhouse kitchen, all unpretentious design, pine tables and chairs, deep porcelain sink, and simple yet elegant lines. She couldn't take her eyes off of the professional-grade stove that was a focal point. It was painted a deep forest green and sported six cast iron burners.

Liz caught Martha's gaze and gave a laugh. "My pride and joy and a *total* indulgence, even though I don't cook much anymore," she said. "I saw it and couldn't resist."

She placed an earthen mug in front of Martha, who'd taken a seat on a small stool at the kitchen island. Martha guessed from the aroma that it was some kind of French roast.

Taking a sip from her own mug and leaning back against the counter, Liz asked, "So what brings you out here so early in the morning?"

"I'm actually here about Carla Innsbruck," Martha said. "Did you know her? They've arrested my friend for her murder and I'm trying to gather any facts that might help the police start looking in the right direction and away from her."

"Didn't know her at all," Liz replied. "And the police already talked to me. As you know, I was one of the few people at the church when she was killed. I explained to them that we were all in and out of the Fellowship Hall, that I had no previous connection to her, and that I had no useful information. They told me to stay in town, and I said that was no problem since my only plans were those related to the retreat and finishing up a few things here. With all the contractors I've got coming and going, *I'm* going absolutely nowhere."

"Are you new to the area?" Martha asked. Though she'd met Liz the night of the keynote, they'd mainly talked about the upcoming retreat events, nothing personal.

"Yes and no," Liz replied. "I grew up around Adair, but moved here after my parents died. I lived in New Hampshire for most of my adult life, raised my kids up there, lost my husband there. Once I realized that my kids were likely not going to settle back in New Hampshire after they graduated from college, I decided to move back here and start afresh." Her eyes moved around the kitchen. "It's exciting and strange all at the same time. But mostly it suits me just fine. Of course, it's easy to start again when you have resources."

Martha couldn't help but be attracted to Liz's openness and humility. "Wow. I have to admit, I may have had the wrong first impression of you."

"Oh, that. I must come across as a big B because you're not the first person to think that way. Must be all those years of living in the northeast. You eventually develop an RBF just to get through the cold, the rat race, the cost of living, the whole thing."

"Ah." Martha nodded. *Resting bitch face.* "Say no more. I lived in Boston for over twenty years before moving back to Riley Creek, so I get it. I actually stopped by to ask about your opinion piece on Carla that came out yesterday. It was pretty... harsh for someone who didn't really know her."

"Ah, yes. The article. Is it OK if we move to the table?" Both women walked over to a rustic pine dining table that sat in a windowed nook. Martha sat on a long black bench that ran the length of one side of the table and Liz took a seat in a matching black Windsor-style chair across from her.

Liz took up the story. "Martha, I'm sixty-five years old. I figure I've got about twenty good years left, maybe a few more. Everyone in my family is deceased, except for my kids who are just starting their own lives and own adventures. Oh, and my brother-in-law who is perpetually broke and after me to go into one ill-conceived business venture after another with him. After my mother died and I realized the kids weren't moving back home, I had a good think about what it was I wanted to spend these last twenty years doing. And I came up with two things that are really important to me: writing and the environment.

"See, I graduated from the University of Missouri, one of the best journalism schools in the country. But my writing career was a short one once I married Rob and our kids started arriving. One of us had to give up our career and it was simple: he made more money. So I took on the caregiver role and that was that.

"Fast forward thirty-plus years and here we are. I'm building this LEED certified house and trying my hand again at some free-lance writing." She shrugged and nodded across the room to a tiny nook that Martha hadn't noticed. It housed a small desk that folded down from the wall. On it sat a laptop, a pair of folded glasses, and a pile of papers and books.

"What's LEED certified?" Martha asked, making small talk while her mind raced. "I know it's something about being energy efficient, right?"

"Yes, and even more than that. It's designing a home to maximize fresh air, water and energy conservation, using healthy building materials. There's a lot more that goes into it, but those are some of the highlights. It's kind of fun, really. I can do things like set the thermostat using an app on my phone, and my fridge"—here she gestured over her shoulder at a fridge with a window in the front—"lights up when I tap that window twice. It decreases the energy loss that comes from me opening the door to stand and stare at its contents. Isn't that *wild*?"

"Sure is," said Martha. "But... the article?"

"Oh yes, right. Get to the point, Liz." She laughed. "The article is me getting back to the second thing I want to spend those twenty years on: writing and, more specifically, journalism. You may find it terribly opportunistic, but when I heard about Innsbruck's death, I called up the local paper, explained I was an ex-journalist and attending the retreat, and offered to write a short piece about the keynote. I may have embellished it a bit, but honestly, what she was proposing *was* pretty offensive. Like I told the police when I talked to them, I had no personal relationship to her. I was just writing it as I saw it." She paused, then added, "But I re-read it today and... I'm thinking I *am* a bit rusty and could have softened it up."

Martha couldn't see how this calm, open personality could have stuck a knife into Carla so, unable to come up with any more questions, she thanked Liz for the coffee, complimented her again on her home, and returned to her car. On the way back to Riley Creek, she rolled down the window to let Penny stick her nose out and take in the spring air. Several times, the terrier took in too much air and fell into a sneezing fit.

"Too much of a good thing, huh?" Martha asked Penny, just before the dog stuck her snout right back out the window.

A cardinal's "birdie, birdie, birdie" call sounded from the clock as Martha and Penny strolled in through the shop's back door. Ten o'clock. Penny raced up the stairs to the office while Martha joined

PJ, Helen, and Margaret who were all gathered around an open laptop computer that sat on the counter.

"What's everybody looking at?" Martha asked, coming around the counter to see the laptop's screen.

"I'll be darned," said Helen in her usual understated way.

"Holy crap, Martha! We just made five sales through the website. In the past hour," PJ boomed. "Apparently, each shopper 'liked' one of the photos we put up on the website, then placed an order for Fly Buy Beans. So far, we've got orders for two bags of Sumatran Migration, three bags of Brazilian Tailfeather, and four bags of Rufous Blend."

"All that from just adding some photos?" Martha asked incredulously.

"Well, partly, but maybe also because we've been taking some... creative liberties." PJ glanced at Margaret and Helen. Margaret pushed up her kitty cat glasses, swallowed hard, and backed up until she had enough space to turn and dart to her usual table where a teacup, saucer, and laptop sat. There, she made herself invisible behind her screen. Helen looked over to the bird merchandise, mumbled something about restocking, and nearly ran behind a rack of mugs.

Martha looked questioningly at PJ. "Um, am I missing something?" she asked.

"Now, honey—"

Martha put her hands on her hips. "OK, PJ. Anytime Aunt Lorna started a sentence with 'Now, honey,' I knew I wasn't going to like what came after. What's going on?"

"Well, honey, you know Joanne and Margaret know much more about this whole 'doing business online' thing than we do. Joanne set up your website to show all of your coffees, and the two of them suggested we make a Facebook page. Well, the Facebook page Joanne made takes people right to the website where they can order our coffee. So, we all got to thinking about what would make people pay more attention to our Facebook page and click on the website to order coffee. It was Margaret, actually, who came up with the idea of telling more of your story."

PJ and Martha looked over to Margaret. The older woman was so completely hidden behind her computer that she existed merely as a pair of black-jeaned legs ending in black Chuck Taylors.

"What do you mean, 'telling my story'?" Martha asked suspiciously.

"Well... here." PJ pushed the laptop closer to Martha and she took a look. She scanned the links to the store's hours, a small square of map showing its location, a menu of coffees. But it was the photo across the top of the page that caught her eye. It showed Martha and Aunt Lorna from a few years ago, standing in front of the shop, smiling with their arms around one another. A banner superimposed across their midsections read "Gone, but never forgotten." Martha clicked on the "About" tab and found an abridged story of her decision to take over ownership of the shop and how she was trying to make a go of the struggling business.

"*What*?" she said to PJ, projecting the word out to the shop so that her anger could comfortably encompass Margaret and Helen too. "How dare you three put my personal business out there like that! To sell coffee? What were you *thinking*?"

The clicking of Penny's nails sounded as she came across the floor to Martha's side, attentive to her mood even from afar.

"Now, honey—"

"Don't 'now honey' me, PJ. This is really too much. You never even asked me my opinion of this before you did it. You know I value my privacy and would never have allowed you to trade on it in the name of retail."

"Don't blame PJ," came a small squeak of a voice. "It was my idea." Margaret had slipped out from behind her computer and was slinking back over to the counter.

"Mine too," came Helen's voice as she joined Margaret. Both looked chastened.

Margaret cleared her throat and said, "You know how shy I am. I find it very uncomfortable to be the center of attention in any way. But to sell any of my books, I've had to allow my publisher to publicize, and that has meant allowing her to tell readers a bit more about me than I'd normally be comfortable with. The result has been more books sold than I'd ever thought possible."

Margaret's efforts had caused her to turn beet red. Helen stepped in.

"She's right, Martha. I know you're upset, but we wanted to show you what was possible if we really put both feet into the on-line marketing world. Joanne did most of the technical work, but she also taught us that in order to compete, we had to help people *understand* Birds 'n' Beans. Then maybe they'd go to our Fly Buy Beans website and spend money. We tried to talk to Lorna about this when she was alive, but you know her. She was like a brick wall. Perhaps we shouldn't have done it, but we wanted you to see what could happen before you said no to the whole thing."

A soft 'bing' sounded from the laptop. PJ turned the screen and clicked on the touchpad.

"Someone has sent a message to the Facebook page." She leaned in to read. "They're asking if we sell bird-friendly coffee."

Helen sighed. "As usual, the answer is no."

Martha set aside her anger for a moment and said, "What do you mean, 'as usual'?"

"Your Aunt Lorna was a wonderful friend to me, but she could be as stubborn as a mule," PJ began. "For the last few years, we've had lots of requests to sell bird-friendly coffee. Helen, can you explain it?"

"Sure," Helen said. "You know when you go to the store and see bags of coffee stamped with all kinds of certifications? Like certified shade-grown, certified organic, and so on? Well, the bird-friendly certification is a very strict one, requiring the beans to be organic—no pesticides used in their farming—and shade-grown, which means a certain level of canopy is required, encouraging more natural habitat for birds. It's a bit more work to source, so costs a bit more. Lorna had her mind on so many other things the last year or so of her life, we just couldn't get her to consider making a change in our beans and buying all bird-friendly. So anytime someone has asked if we sell bird-friendly coffee, we've had to say no."

Martha pondered this. "Well, I've had it mentioned twice to me in the last two days, and this Facebook question makes three times. If our customers are asking, we've got to think about this. Would you two be willing to investigate it for me?"

Helen and PJ exchanged glances. "Already have," Helen said. "We've identified a bird-friendly coffee farm we'd love to order our beans from."

Martha looked at the laptop, then at her three friends.

"What's that saying? In for a penny, in for a pound? Not sure we can run a shop called Birds 'n' Beans without doing our part to take care of the birds. Let's buy some bird-friendly beans, roast them up, and see how they do. Let's try it!" Nodding back to the laptop, she winked at her friends and said, "And let's get those orders filled."

New Canaan, Tennessee, United States, August 1, 1891

IT IS AS HOT TODAY as if Satan himself had opened up the Earth and stoked the fires of Hell so that we could more closely feel the burn. Thomas and I don't even need to strain a muscle to be drenched in sweat. If Bell could invent a machine to make the voice travel, surely someday someone will invent a machine to help us escape this hellish Tennessee heat!

It's been decided: our new shared home will be called Double Oaks. We finished clearing the land midsummer and have been putting in the foundation over the past month. In two weeks, our friends and neighbors will help us with the framing and roof, and by late fall, Thomas, Susannah and I should be able to move into our permanent home. This is exactly what I dreamed of so many months ago when I set sail from England: a community that I am truly a part of creating with my own two hands.

The library is set to open this winter. Susannah remains busy planning the opening ceremony, which is to include dignitaries from neighboring towns. So far, she says she has catalogued over 2,000 volumes ranging from home economics to world affairs, and she expects the collection to grow significantly as more donations arrive. She allowed Thomas and me a peek a few weeks ago, and indeed it is a structure we can all take great pride in. Its tall windows bring in the sun all day long, and two reading tables with chairs stretch almost the length of the room. A ladder rolls along the shelves, allowing patrons and Susannah to browse the collection. She even dreams of hosting small poetry readings in the back near the river, the ring of six boulders there forming a natural staging area. What is it about a library that gives the body of a town its beating heart?

New Canaan now boasts a church, a school, a post office, an inn, a library, a cemetery, a sawmill, and a mercantile. Most of its other structures are private dwellings, and these seem to multiply like bugs. Our young people—some of whom arrived with more resources than others—have started social clubs, theatrical events, and even a newspaper of sorts. I know these are a natural occurrence, part of the evolution of a town, but I confess that I am frustrated that some of these individuals feel no call to participate in the hard labor required to advance the town before another winter sets in. It seems to me that the lower and middle classes do the work here and the wealthy enjoy themselves, much as it was back in England. Some things we still need to unlearn, and I trust we will, in time.

It has been nice to have Susannah with us. Some of our neighbors call us The Three Musketeers! Last week, she and I walked down to the river after church. Thomas had promised Mr. Peterson to help him re-shoe a mare, so he remained behind. It was a magical afternoon, one I have pondered greatly on since.

Being with Susannah is much like being at home with some of my school friends. Her English is nearly perfect now, and we talk about books and music. I confess that my fondness for her is growing, but I dare not allow it to. Thomas has mentioned to me several times that she is far too young to consider walking out with anyone, and I sense my romantic interest in his sister would not be welcomed. I shall focus on our friendship and on the future, which will have us living, as friends, under the same roof.

Chapter Nine

M artha left Penny asleep in her upstairs bed and walked through the square to Elder's Hardware. She entered and spotted Frank putting a brown plastic bottle that she guessed was hydrogen peroxide and a box of Band-Aids in a bag, and handing it to Karen Todd, the retreat participant Martha had met at the Fellowship Hall.

"Hey, Karen," she said as their paths met.

"Hi, Martha," Karen replied.

"Finding some good hardware to help with your writing?" Martha asked with a small laugh, gesturing at the bag.

"Oh yes, you never know what you'll need when you're out in the woods for a few days." The other woman smiled. "Just picking up some things to treat a bunch of paper cuts," she said, gesturing at her bag. "I really need to graduate to writing on a computer, but I'm still pretty old school."

"You're not too far from home, though, right? Johnson City, I think you said. Is that where you live?"

"Yep, my husband and I live there. Have done for years," Karen replied.

"Little Chicago!" Martha laughed.

Karen looked confused, but then laughed back. "Yep, well, it's not quite Chicago yet, but it's on its way."

Martha frowned at Karen's back as she left the store, but shook it off and went to talk to Frank.

"Hey, Martha. How are you? Have you found anything out yet that can help Mary Jane?" he asked anxiously. She could see he had not slept much the night before.

"I'm working on it, Frank. You said you'd give me the name of the contractor."

"Yeah. His name is Scott DeLuca and he'll be out at Liz Waterson's by eleven this morning."

"That's weird. I was actually just out there," Martha said, checking her watch. She had time for a quick trip out to Rhubarb Pike, and then back for the author critiques after lunch. "By the way, have you heard any more from Albert?"

"He called this morning. They may charge her with murder later today, but so far they're holding her on suspicion of murder and plan to question her again this afternoon. They let me and Ethel Jean bring over some clean clothes and reading materials last night."

The thought of her friend reading in a lonely cell made Martha's heart cringe. "OK. Well, I'd better get back out to Liz's place to catch Scott. Thanks again, Frank, and hang in there." She reached out and squeezed his hand.

Frank leaned in a bit. "Oh, and for what it's worth, don't pay any attention to anyone who's been complaining about this retreat. I've seen several writers, men and women, going into Clint and Tara's places for haircuts, and I can't keep pocketknives and Riley Creek baseball caps and t-shirts on the shelves. Turns out this was a great idea for the village."

Martha smiled. *Well, that is one piece of good news.*

She exited the hardware store just as Officer Daniels was parking his police cruiser in a nearby spot. She waited as he got out of the vehicle, holding a hand up to her forehead to shield her eyes from the sun.

"Hi there, Chip!" she called.

Officer Daniels appeared to look around the square, then gave a meager wave and came her way.

"Hello, Ms. Sloane," he said politely.

"Oh, you know you can call me Martha."

"I'm afraid I'd better keep it professional, what with your friend being in jail for the murder," he all but mumbled.

"Chip, you know Mary Jane had nothing to do with Carla's murder. You know her better than that."

"Well, I do find it hard to believe..." he trailed off. "But the chief..."

Martha felt her anger flare. "Your chief has his head up his... he is just crazy if he thinks she has anything to do with it. And I'm going to prove it."

"That's just the thing, Ms. Sloane," he said, sounding reluctant. He removed his hat. "The chief says I'm to report anything I see you doing that looks suspicious. See, he talked to Carla Innsbruck's ex yesterday and found out you'd already talked to him. He was pretty angry. Thinks you're investigating on your own... again. Which it sounds like you are." This last sentence, Chip said with a gulp.

"You can tell your chief that you saw me coming out of the hardware store where I'd been *investigating* some new *hardware* for my *toilet tank*. That should teach him to keep his nose out of my business."

Martha walked back to her Subaru behind the shop and headed once again to Rhubarb Pike, fuming. The nerve of Teddy Perry to tell his officer to keep an eye on her!

This time, she found Liz's place immediately and parked along the roadside. She got out and walked up the driveway to the garage where she saw a contractor's van parked, ladders affixed to the top and tools spilling from the open back doors. All of the garage doors were open and she spotted a man on a ladder affixing an electrical box to the ceiling.

"Scott?" she called. "I'm Martha Sloane, a friend of Frank Elder. Do you have a minute to talk?"

The man on the ladder turned his screwdriver a couple of rotations before replying, "Yep, that's me," and climbing down to stand next to her. "I told Frank I don't really want to get involved in anything related to that crazy lady getting murdered."

"I'm not asking you to get involved, just to answer a few questions that might help get Frank's girlfriend freed from prison. She's a close friend of mine and I guarantee you she had nothing to do with the murder."

Scott pushed his ball cap back on his forehead. "Yeah, Frank told me about Mary Jane. You're right—no way was she involved in anything. That woman is a saint as far as I'm concerned. She helped my wife a few months back when she had car trouble out on Route 2. Tell me what you want to know."

"Well, I understand you put Mary Jane in touch with Carla Innsbruck. Can you tell me more about that?"

"Well, there's not much *to* tell," Scott said. "I was at Ms. Innsbruck's place over in Adair. She had a skylight on the back side of the house, and I was patching a spot along the side that was causing her to have a leak any time it rains. She really needed a new roof, but told me she couldn't afford one just yet.

"Anyway, while I'm up there working, a car pulls in. Next thing I know, Ms. Innsbruck and some other woman are having a huge blowout. I wasn't eavesdropping, mind you, but I heard the other woman say something about 'Ivan's gonna kill you if you don't stop all of your nature walks and start delivering on that manuscript' and Ms. Innsbruck told the other woman that Ivan could kiss her a—" He stopped himself. "You get the idea."

"Yes, I think I can fill in the blanks." Martha nodded encouragingly. This was the first real lead she'd had since she started looking into Carla's murder. *Someone saying someone else was going to kill her? Manna from heaven.*

"They went on like that for a few minutes, the other lady telling Ms. Innsbruck how much they all needed the money, Ms. Innsbruck saying how she didn't want to get back into the publishing circus. Round and round they went. Finally, the other lady slammed out, got in her car, and left. I was curious about who Ms. Innsbruck was so I googled her, from right up there on her roof. Turns out she was sort of a famous writer back in the day. I happened to mention it to Frank the next week, and a few days later, he calls to ask me her phone number. That's really all I know."

Martha was anxious to get back to the village, help with the author critiques, then find out more about Carla's publisher. She thanked Scott and turned to walk back to her car.

"Not that it's any of my business, but do you know who you should really be talking to?" Scott asked conspiratorially. "That one." He gestured with his head toward the house.

"Liz Waterson? Do you mean about the editorial?" Martha asked. "Already did. She explained why she wrote such a scathing piece."

"I don't know about any editorial. I just know the two of them got into it last week. Right up there on that porch. My daughter was here working with me, planting some bushes on the side of the house, and heard the whole thing. Ms. Innsbruck called Ms. Waterson a 'wannabe greenie' who claimed to protect the Earth while cutting down trees to make way for her own McMansion. Told Ms. Waterson she'd seen her kind a million times, and then marched off."

Martha checked her watch and knew she didn't have time right now to talk to Liz about this new information. She only just had time to get back for the critiques, so she thanked Scott again and promised herself she'd follow up with Liz. Why hadn't she mentioned this run-in with Carla?

Martha drove faster than usual on her way back to Riley Creek. The writers would be gathering at Toad in a Hole and she'd promised Octavius that she'd be on hand to help. Not that she knew anything about chapter critiques, but as President of the R-C and the person who'd dreamed up the retreat, she felt obligated to help in any way to make the weekend a success.

She parked on the street and hurried into the shop. Already the writers had pulled groups of chairs together and were huddled and talking, some with sheaves of paper in hand and some holding laptops. Octavius had wisely put on some gentle classical music to play in the background, and the mood in the room felt friendly.

Margaret and Octavius were arranging coffee and cookies on a side table and greeted Martha when she approached.

"Sorry I'm late! Things look like they're going well here," she said brightly.

"Indeed," Octavius nodded in agreement. "And on a selfish note, I'm happy to report that I've sold several thesauruses and just as many bird identification books over the last day." A broad grin spread across his face.

Margaret shyly excused herself, explaining that one of the critique groups had agreed to let her join. Martha and Octavius watched as she took her laptop out from behind the checkout desk and pulled up a chair to join Angie, Nick, Liz, and Karen.

"Is it just me or is that the exact same group that was in the Fellowship Hall the night Carla was killed?" Martha asked Octavius.

Octavius's grin faded. "Indeed it is. Margaret tells me they've named themselves the 'Murder Squad' and have become quite friendly."

Martha felt queasy. This was *not* the bonding between artists enthralled with the written word she'd envisioned for the weekend.

They stood quietly for a few more minutes, then Martha broke the silence. "Octavius, if you think things are under control here, would you mind very much if I slipped over to the shop to make some calls? I learned some new information about Carla this morning that I'd like to look into. I shouldn't be too long."

Octavius encouraged her to go, so she made a beeline for Birds 'n' Beans.

Martha entered the shop through the front and nearly collided with Helen who had just come down the stairs holding an armful of boxes.

"Whoa! What's all that?" Martha asked.

"Online orders to go out with the next UPS pickup," Helen said, sounding breathless and excited. "We're taking everything over to Silent Sisters 'cause Ethel Jean has a pickup already scheduled."

Incredulous, Martha followed her tall friend through the hallway that connected Birds 'n' Beans to Silent Sisters. Ethel Jean was behind the register, using packing tape to seal a large box. Helen stacked the boxes near the front door, gave Ethel Jean a wave and headed back to Birds 'n' Beans.

"Sounds like that online business of yours is taking off," Ethel Jean said gruffly.

"Well, no real thanks to me," Martha replied. "It's mostly Joanne's technical know-how and PJ, Helen, and Margaret's marketing ideas."

"Yeah, but it's you who encouraged them to go for it. Much as I loved your aunt, she never wanted to do things differently." Ethel Jean looked down at the box she'd been taping up. "I guess now I'll have to take a page from your stupid book and get more creative. Right now, I'm packing up these first editions for one of those writers of yours, Liz Waterson. Woman has money to burn, apparently."

Martha whistled. "Whew! Your first editions cost a pretty penny."

"And to think it's my sister who insists we buy those old books and she's not even here to enjoy the sale." At the mention of Mary Jane, Ethel Jean's face gave in and tears welled in her eyes. "She drives me damn nuts, but I can't stand the thought of her in that jail cell. How can that idiot boyfriend of yours really think she had anything to do with that woman's murder?"

"I don't know, Ethel Jean. I suppose he's just doing his job. But I know it'll all get figured out and she'll be out of there soon. And remember, she's got Albert on her side."

"Well, that's something, I suppose." Ethel Jean sniffed. Pulling herself up to her full five-foot-three, the older woman sobered and pointed her short finger in Martha's face. "*You'd* better get her out of there, and *SOON*." She turned away and Martha knew she'd been dismissed.

Martha walked back through the hall and up the stairs to the office. Penny lifted her ears, excited to see Martha, but not excited enough to get up from her cozy bed. Martha patted her head and gave her ears a scratch, then settled in at the computer. It didn't take her many minutes of internet searching to find Carla Innsbruck's editor from before she went to prison.

Ivan Gregory of Inland Books had published four of her titles, two of them having made the bestseller list back in the early 2000s. Inland Books looked to have shrunk to just a handful of titles per year, and boasted only two other staff in addition to Gregory. One was named Sherry! Though no address was listed on the website, a phone number Martha recognized as having a Nashville prefix was.

She dialed. After two rings, a very young and very bored voice sounded.

"Inland Books. Can I help you?" After asking for Ivan Gregory, Martha was placed on an abrupt hold.

The line picked up again. "Gregory," came a deep and clipped voice.

Martha identified herself and politely expressed her condolences over the recent passing of Mr. Gregory's former client, Carla Innsbruck.

"*Hmmph. Very* former client, that is. Thanks, but she hadn't produced anything with us for years, and now she's really left us in the lurch," he said angrily.

Martha had been halfheartedly clicking around on Inland Books' website when Gregory had come on the line. She suddenly sat up, looking more closely at the image on her laptop screen. *This* was Gregory? She recognized him as having accepted one of the floral arrangements at the end of Carla's keynote. His slicked-back black hair with silver at the temples was very distinctive, as was his sallow skin. He could have doubled for a sixty-something Bela Lugosi.

"Were you in Riley Creek a couple of evenings ago? The evening she was... killed here?" Martha asked.

"Yes, but I got out of there fast at the end. The whole thing was a disaster." Did he mean the keynote or Carla's murder?

Martha explained, perhaps stretching the truth a bit, that she was assisting the local police with their inquiries. She asked if he'd been in touch with Carla lately.

"*In touch*? You'd better believe I've been in touch. That woman owed me a manuscript for her autobiography *months* ago and I haven't seen so much as a chapter out of her. One of our editors, Sherry, lives up in your area and had even gone over to Carla's falling down house to try to get it out of her, but she said Carla was more interested in mapping out hikes outside of the state park than doing any writing. We were hoping this keynote gig might whet her appetite for publicity and shake the manuscript out of her. What a total backfire."

Martha took the opportunity to ask Gregory for Sherry's phone number and address and noted it down.

"Do you and Sherry have an office in Nashville?" she asked.

"Are you kidding me? Do you know how much office space in Nashville costs? Hardly any publisher I know has actual office space anymore. No, we all work from home. It works, but I tell ya', I sure miss the old days."

"Have you always been Carla's publisher?"

"Yep, but in the good old days—like I was just talking about when we had an actual copy machine and lunch room and office to go to—she cranked out manuscripts like water, and we turned around and sold them like hotcakes. I think the old girl lost her touch when she went to prison. We haven't even seen her in years. She is—was—months late with anything I could use to even start doing marketing kits. I don't know what was going on with her, and now I guess we'll never know. She went from an environmentalist to a 'kill the Earth' quack. And now I'll never get my manuscript. I guess her backlist might have a spike from all the PR."

Martha paused, and then said rather tentatively, "You don't sound very upset by Carla's murder, Mr. Gregory."

The man on the other end of the phone seemed to snap out of his calculation of backlist profits. "Oh, don't get me wrong. I am. Of course I am. But you have to understand, the publishing business is tough right now, far worse than it's ever been. We were *all* counting on the income from that autobiography and she's been making us crazy by delaying and delaying on the manuscript. She was a gifted writer and could rally people around a cause like nobody's business, but when she got her mind stuck on something, there was just no budging her. And it seemed like lately she'd been stuck on something other than turning in this manuscript."

New Canaan, Tennessee, United States, December 7, 1891

IT IS HARD TO BELIEVE that almost two years have passed since I first imagined a life beyond England. Yet here I am, a man on the verge of having everything he ever dreamed of, and facing my second New Canaan winter. Thank God—thus far, it is not so bitter as the last.

Much has changed since I last sat down to fill these pages. Most importantly, Double Oaks has moved from a dream to an almost completed reality. We raised the walls in November and the roof will be complete in another week. A bit later than we'd hoped, but still in time to shelter us from the bitter winds. While the men have worked like ants to complete the exterior, Susannah and other women from the community made the inside a home, adding horse hair and hay into the walls to insulate against the coming cold. It is dirty and difficult work and I credit these women with the strength of sturdy men.

The three of us have very few possessions to speak of; what furniture we have has been donated by our friends or purchased on credit. Mr. Daniels, the carpenter, has constructed fine beds for all of us and a dinner table besides. We will place it in Thomas and Susannah's kitchen and share it until we can purchase a second one for my side of the house.

Susannah and I have taken to meeting privately, going to elaborate lengths to make these meetings appear coincidental. We make frequent trips to the mercantile where we "decide" to walk back to Double Oaks together. Thomas often skips church on Sunday, whereas I have become a dedicated attendee, and Susannah and I walk home togeth-

er. Thomas has made his feelings on the topic of his sister known to me: she is too young to be betrothed and needs to marry into another German family. Yet I am as a firefly to a lantern and could fill this page reflecting on the color of Susannah's hair.

We have been circumspect in stating our feelings for one another, but I feel sure she returns my affection. She is a good sister and does not wish to vex her brother, yet she shows up in the places she knows I frequent and seems to have a book at the ready for me when I come to the library in need of reading material. I have become a most voracious reader in the past few months.

Thomas cannot know of all the time Susannah and I spend together, though his attitude toward me seems markedly changed. Yesterday, as we rode hay out to the cattle, he said very little. I asked him what was the matter and he claimed a headache. I hope that is the case and that it is not Susannah coming between us.

Already I dread the winter to come, when we will all be kept to our houses with fewer reasons to venture out for leisurely walks and chance encounters. I hope that the library will stay open no matter the weather. We villagers must remain true to our educations, after all.

Still no word on the train spur. We ask Mr. Hicks for updates whenever we see him, and he tells us he is awaiting word from the rail company executives and our supporters in Boston. His worried brow does not escape our notice.

Chapter Ten

Martha ended her call with Ivan Gregory, thought for a moment, then dialed Teddy's number. She was still steamed at him for arresting Mary Jane, so when he picked up, she practiced an aloof tone.

"I'm glad you called," he said.

"I am merely calling to report that I *may* be able to get you Sherry Newcomb's address by later this afternoon. I spoke with someone who knows her and I'll pass it on as soon as I have it."

"Martha, I—"

"Goodbye, Chief Perry," Martha said, before disconnecting the call with a touch of her index finger.

Martha roused Penny with an enthusiastic "C'mon, Pen!" and they were out the door and in the car, heading for the cottage. While Penny scouted around the enclosed front garden, Martha gathered up everything she'd need for a hike and stuffed it into her daypack: binoculars, a topographical map of the area around the state park, a few granola bars and enough water for both her and Penny, and a bandana. After throwing on her light hiking pants, a ball cap and her Keen hiking shoes, she hopped back into the Subaru with Penny springing in behind her.

Before leaving the small gravel driveway and reliable internet signal, she glanced on her phone at the directions to Sherry Newcomb's home. It took them forty minutes to reach her house in Adair, a modest duplex in a neighborhood of modest duplexes.

Penny was less grumpy than usual about staying in the car, and she curled up for a nap as Martha exited the station wagon.

Sherry opened the door on the first knock, seeming unsurprised to see Martha. Short with medium-length brown hair, some blonde streaks showing through, Sherry wore jeans, sneakers, and a turquoise three-quarter-sleeve V-neck t-shirt.

"Ivan called me," she said. "I figured it was either you or the police wanting to talk with me."

"I suspect you'll get a visit from the police later today. They'll want to know more about Carla and anything you saw after the keynote before you left the church."

"Well, I won't have much to tell them. They've been calling and calling, and I haven't picked up. I'm too upset to talk to them. I left with most of the other ticked-off attendees; I had no *idea* she was going to say what she said, and I needed to calm Ivan down before he headed back to Nashville."

"So neither of you stayed behind with Carla?" Martha asked.

"Are you *kidding*? Did you see the faces on that crowd of people? All we could think about was damage control, and how the keynote would impact her autobiography—assuming she was ever going to actually *submit* the manuscript, of course."

"Why did she say yes to the keynote? And how did you not know what she was going to say?"

Sherry scoffed. "You obviously don't know Carla. She kept herself to herself, and shared nothing about her writing until she felt like sharing it. Same goes for her keynote remarks, apparently. I'm newer to Inland, but Ivan's been there since the beginning and he says Carla was always stubborn and secretive about her drafts. Just not so secretive that he thought she'd take a 180-degree turn away from every public stance on the environment she'd ever had." Sherry threw up her hands.

"How did you end up helping to organize the keynote?"

"Well, our contact in Riley Creek, Mary Jo someone—"

"Mary *Jane*. That's my *friend* Mary Jane you're referring to," Martha blurted more abruptly than she'd intended.

"Yes, sorry. Mary Jane got Carla's number from some workman who'd been patching her roof, and called to invite her. Carla didn't want to do it, so referred Mary Jane to me. After much cajoling from me, Carla decided that she needed the money too much to turn the invitation down. Privately, Ivan and I hoped that the experience might jolt her into turning in the manuscript for her autobiography that she'd been promising us for months. You know, a little attention from her adoring fans?" In a more serious voice, she said, "Guess that didn't work out as we'd planned."

"What do you think happened? How did the keynote go so far off the rails? Did she seem concerned about anything? Might she have been ill?"

"I've been racking my brains over that," Sherry said. "It never occurred to me to ask her what she was going to say. I just figured it would be a variation on her usual theme: protect the Earth, down with the development, et cetera. Sure, she'd been more focused on the woods than on words lately, but I never dreamed... and as for how she seemed... she seemed like the cat that ate the canary. Like she was about to get one over on someone. If you know what I mean. Well, I guess the joke was on Carla."

"What do you mean, 'focused on the woods?'" Martha queried, ignoring the rest of the woman's commentary.

"The last time I was at her house, she'd been poring over a map. I think it was a map of the state park. She'd drawn on it with a thick black magic marker, and had put some Xs on it too. Probably for some crazy nature poetry or something. Who knows?" Sherry shrugged dismissively.

"Sherry, if I showed you a map, do you think you could point out the general area she'd marked on her map?" Martha wasn't sure what this would prove, but it felt important somehow.

"Sure, I guess. I can try," Sherry said doubtfully.

Martha zipped out to the car, grabbed her map and a red pen from the glove box, and popped back into the townhouse. She spread the map out across Sherry's kitchen table.

Sherry looked at the map, cocking her head this way and that. Turning it, she said, "Ah, there we go. That's how she had it." She accepted the pen from Martha, and slowly drew a circle around an area on the eastern side of the campground. Standing back and looking down at the map, Sherry nodded and said, "Yep, that looks just like hers. That's the spot she was studying."

Martha peered closely at the circle. Looking down just slightly so she could see her watch but not appear rude, she realized that she could be there in thirty minutes if she left now, and still be back at the shop by mid-afternoon. Parting from Sherry with a promise from her to call if she thought of anything else, Martha fast-walked to the car and nearly screeched out of the duplex's parking lot.

Penny stood up in the passenger seat and looked straight at Martha as if to say, "Woman, *really*?"

"I know, I know. Sorry. But I think we're onto something here. I have no idea what, but *something*." Sensing Martha's excitement, Penny spent the rest of the drive sitting straight up with her rectangular muzzle pointing ahead.

Pulling into the guest parking area near the entrance to the Paris River State Park, Martha shouldered her pack and clipped on

Penny's recycled climbing rope dog leash. Immediately to the right of the parking lot was a small wooden kiosk housing a trail map behind a plastic cover and offering free paper maps to take along. Just beyond the kiosk stood a wooden sign listing multiple trail names with arrows pointing this way and that. Martha consulted the red circle Sherry had made, studied the list of trails, and selected the one that veered the furthest east.

Within a few minutes, she and Penny had fallen into an easy rhythm. Martha realized she'd been holding herself tight as a drum all the way from Sherry's, and the spicy smell of wet leaves mingled with the fresh spring air made her relax and pace herself. The afternoon sun cut through the canopy in dusty golden rays. She began paying more attention to the plants emerging along the trailside and felt a little thrill when she recognized the wildflowers.

First to catch her eye were her favorites, little brown jugs. She thought initially it might be a wild ginger plant because of its shiny green leaves, but the arrow shape of them suggested it was what she'd hoped. To confirm, she lifted the plant's leaves and sure enough: settled in the base of the plant's stems were a cluster of five fleshy jug shapes.

Next, she spotted the wavy-lobed leaves of a patch of bloodroot, a few short stems emerging. Though the flowers' petals were closed up tight, she knew once the afternoon sun hit them, they would unfurl into beautiful white blooms. She sent up silent thanks to Aunt Lorna, who had taught her that bloodroot took its name from the red-orange sap that Native Americans found several uses for.

She was happily surprised that she remembered the names of so many of the wildflowers she saw. Noticing the telltale splotches on the trout lily leaves, she made a promise to herself to come back in a few weeks to catch their yellow blooms. She detected several patches of three-leaved trillium, but until they flowered, it would be hard to tell if they were white, yellow, or red. Feeling like a snorkeler stumbling on a trunk of doubloons in a shipwreck, she knew she would be back with her camera.

Keeping Penny on the trail so she didn't accidentally drop a paw onto a tender wildflower, Martha kept moving along. As she came around its easternmost side, she sensed the trail veering back westward, but she knew from Sherry's markings that the area she wanted to explore was even further east.

Looking around to make sure there were no other people in sight, she took a deep breath and stepped off the trail. She felt resistance in the leash and looked down at Penny, whose front paw was held in the air as if she were hesitant to leave the established path.

"It's OK this once," Martha encouraged her. "It's just for a few minutes. We need to check something out."

Delicately, the schnauzer took a step and followed Martha. They weaved their way around fallen trees, sink holes, and the odd patch of bear corn, Martha not really sure what they were looking for and trying to detect anything out of the ordinary.

After bushwhacking for ten minutes, Martha noticed Penny's tongue hanging out and decided it was time for a stop. She sat on an enormous fallen tree, unshouldered her pack, and served them both water and some bites of granola bar. Martha took in the sounds of birds, some with songs so elaborate she was sure they must be some kind of warbler. Chewing, she scanned the ground, looking for more wildflowers she could identify.

Maybe Carla was just crazy about the outdoors and marked this area as prime wildflower territory? Just as she was contemplating heading back to the car, she heard Penny sneezing and looked over to her. The terrier was having a sneeze attack from sticking her nose too far into something or other. At the same time, something that didn't belong in this landscape caught Martha's eye. Walking past Penny, she came to a wooden stake in the ground with a bright purple marking whisker nailed to the top.

Over her years working at the university, Martha had been involved in enough groundbreakings with the President to know that a bundle of colored plastic sticks affixed to the top of a stake indicated a boundary of some kind. She stood and put a hand to her forehead as she looked around for another marker. *There.* She found it about fifty yards away.

Packing up the water and snacks, she picked up Penny's leash and began following the stakes. Over the next forty-five minutes, she located enough to encompass most of the area that Sherry had outlined on the map. Whatever it was for, the area was enormous. Tens of acres, far eclipsing the size of any potential nature center she and the other local people had been led to believe the land—if it were to be developed—would be used for.

What are these stakes here for? Martha had no idea, but her Spidey-senses were tingling. *Why was Carla giving this area so much attention?*

Checking her watch, Martha knew she had time to get back to her car, head to the shop to say hi, and still have part of her evening left. Using her phone to take a few pictures of the boundary markers and general area, she then stowed it away in a side pocket of her backpack and led Penny to the main trail. From there, they walked briskly all the way back to the car, not stopping this time to enjoy any trailside fauna.

Martha put her hand on the car door handle and paused. She was only a ten-minute walk from the area in the state park campground where the writers were staying. They would probably still be in the village, but would be coming back soon. Would it hurt to nose around a little bit? She could be checking out the new work on the cabins, if anyone asked.

Martha smiled to herself, then threw her pack in the car, locked it up, and led Penny toward the cabin area along the river. Each cabin looked like the tiny homes she saw on HGTV, and there were new wood railings on several of the attached porches. One bear-proof garbage can sat outside each cabin, and a larger single bear-proof recycling bin sat adjacent to the parking lot.

Martha and Penny casually walked along the empty parking lot, then, with Martha taking a glance around, they slipped to the cabins' backside. Martha peeked in the windows of each one, trying to match the cabin to the writer. Karen's she identified right away, the bottle of hydrogen peroxide and box of Band-Aids she'd seen her with at the hardware store standing on the kitchen table next to a large pot. A few others were so empty of identifying items she could not figure out who was staying where. Angie Bangor's cabin she thought she could identify because of the binoculars hanging from a coat peg. Angie had been one of the few writers to bring her own binoculars to the Intro to Birding night behind Toad in a Hole.

Martha was about to decide that her snooping was pointless when she spotted Nick's wingtips parked on the mat near the front door of the next cabin she peered into. Then her eyes widened. Taped to the walls were rows and rows of blown-up photos of Carla Innsbruck: leaving her house; entering her house; rolling a grocery cart into the Piggly Wiggly; emerging from the liquor store with a small brown bag. A camera with a long lens lay on the kitchen counter.

Martha's heart pounded. *Why in the world would he take so many pictures of Carla?* And then it hit her. *A murderer might have wanted to follow her, to know her movements.*

With a jolt, Martha tugged Penny's leash and they made a beeline back to the Subaru. Hopping in behind Penny, Martha started the wagon up and aimed its nose straight for Riley Creek. Her head was spinning with possibilities, the biggest of which was that Nick had killed Carla in the vestry. She had to calm down to make it safely back home, and then call Teddy.

The route back to the village was winding and beautiful, overhung with branches from the towering trees along the road. Martha slipped a CD in and began humming along to *Red Dirt Girl* to calm her thoughts. Easily rounding the curves in the road and enjoying Emmylou Harris's haunting melodies, she didn't notice the giant black truck until it filled up her rearview mirror.

New Canaan, Tennessee, United States, December 19, 1891

I WRITE TONIGHT BLEAK of heart and low in spirit. Three things have happened which may change my fortunes inexorably; two for the worse and one for the better.

Two nights ago, the inn caught fire. We still do not know what caused the blaze. For three years, she has stood sentinel, embracing newcomer and visitor alike and acting as a grand showpiece for our experimental community.

Thomas and I had been returning from our fields beyond Double Oaks, I thinking only of a wash and then dinner with Susannah, when we caught a strange scent on the air. At almost the same moment, an unfamiliar glow and cloud of black smoke became visible over the trees. We ran, joined by other villagers as the acrid smoke stung our eyes.

It was already too late when we arrived. The entire three floors and grand veranda roiled in smoke, and flames reached out from every broken window. Men ran hither and yon, dumping buckets of water if they could get close, but it was no use. The inn was gone.

Mr. Hicks stood with Pastor Taylor, the clergyman's hand on Mr. Hicks' arm.

"How did this happen?" was all Mr. Hicks said, again and again. "How did this happen?"

Thomas assured him that we would rebuild the inn, and that there were many strong men to do the work.

"There's no money, lad," Mr. Hicks replied. "And without a hotel, any chance we'd had to get the rail line into New Canaan just went up in smoke."

It was hours after the fire that the second tragedy occurred. During the wee morning hours, once the top two floors had crumbled into the first and the flames had died down to clouds of black smoke, I went to find Susannah. I had seen her with the other young women when we'd first arrived, but had not seen her since. I knew she would not have gone back to Double Oaks without Thomas or me, so I went to the library. And indeed she was there, seated at one of the library tables with her head on her folded arms, nearly asleep.

When I entered, she stood and pretended to be alert. Seeing that it was me, she ran into my arms. I spoke to her, trying to calm her, and ran my hands over her hair. Suddenly, the door flew open and a hissing voice sounded.

"As I'd suspected. My very best friend—my brother—taking advantage. You should be ashamed of yourself, Charlton." Thomas, his face blackened from soot and hair sticking out in all directions from under his hat, stood in the doorway.

Susannah and I both spoke, the words tumbling out, proclaiming our love and our intentions toward one another. It came out in all the ways we hadn't wanted it to, and it had the opposite effect than we'd hoped. He turned, disgusted, and ran down the stairs and away.

The third thing, different from the hotel fire and Thomas discovering our secret, was Susannah telling her brother that she loved me and wanted to marry me. I had hoped and dreamed as much, but it was the first time she had said the words. Even as we stood there in the open library door with the smoky cold air rushing in to the cozy space, we embraced as if holding on to each other in a stormy sea.

The night had been a tragedy for New Canaan and, in some ways, for The Three Musketeers, but this moment was, for me, glorious beyond measure. I only hope that in time, Thomas will join in our happiness.

Chapter Eleven

The flash of the truck's chrome rhino bar caught Martha's eye just before it disappeared altogether and rammed the back of her Subaru with a sickening crunch. The car jolted forward and Martha fought to control the wheel. Penny fell down into the footwell and Martha reflexively said, "STAY, PENNY!" in a voice she barely recognized as her own. The schnauzer's ears flattened and she stayed crouching low on the floor of the wagon.

Martha tried to look in the rearview mirror again, but didn't dare take her eyes fully from the winding road ahead. There were no other cars in view, and she heard the truck's engine roar as it prepared for another strike. She put her foot down on the gas pedal and accelerated to as high a rate of speed as she dared. The curves came quickly and she gripped the steering wheel with strained knuckles to keep from losing control. Again, the truck surged forward. Martha sent up thanks laced with profanities as the road straightened out for an extended stretch. She hit the gas. The black truck's driver hit the gas. It jolted forward until it had pulled alongside her, fully taking up the oncoming lane.

She quickly glanced to the left, but tinted windows made it impossible to see the truck's driver. She realized that, unless some miracle happened, she and Penny would be forced into the river that ran along the side of the road and very likely be goners.

The truck's huge black door drew closer.

Martha saw up ahead that the river veered to the right, a wide bank of grass lying between it and the pavement. She accelerated before the truck made contact with her door.

Her memories of the next moment were vague, but she could recall jerking movements, spinning, and the sound of glass breaking. The airbag deployed on her side. Penny yelped in a voice that made Martha's stomach shrivel. Then all was quiet.

Suddenly, Martha felt Penny's tongue licking her face. The terrier's whole body was wiggling and trembling, and Martha felt a lump beginning to form above her silver eyelash.

"It's OK, it's OK," Martha said, not sure it was OK at all, but wanting Penny to know *she* was OK. The sound of the river rushing made Martha sit up. *Ouch.* Her chest hurt.

She looked around. The station wagon was perpendicular to the road, its front tires in the shallows of the river and the rest of it on an incline in the grass. The contents of her purse lay all over the car, and Penny had a bleeding cut on her head. A fine powder filled the air and the deflated air bag drooped around the steering wheel.

Martha focused on the pain in her chest. Putting her hand up, she felt the seatbelt and unbuckled it. Instant relief.

"Where's my phone, Penny?" she asked the terrier. Carefully, and a little shakily, Penny toed her way into the backseat, and then took a tentative hop down to the footwell. Martha could hear her sniffing and scrabbling with her claws. The schnauzer's digging revealed the metallic corner of the phone and Martha managed to twist her body enough to reach it.

"Good job, girl," she said to Penny as she dialed 911.

Teddy looked around, reached inside his breast pocket, and pulled out a small flask. Unscrewing it, he said, "Here, have a sip.

Best thing for shock." Gratefully, Martha took the flask, had a small sip, and grimaced as fire burned from her teeth to her toes.

"Yikes!" she rasped. "Thanks."

"Now, tell me once more. You have *no* idea who it was that ran you off the road?" he asked angrily.

"No, I couldn't see them. It all happened so fast." She sat on the back fender of an ambulance with a silver foil blanket wrapped around her. Penny lay curled up on top of a pillow on the stretcher behind her. "At least she's no worse for wear," Martha tried to laugh as she gestured at the dog. The emergency workers had looked the schnauzer over at Martha's insistence and confirmed the lump on her head did not appear to be anything serious.

"It's not funny," Teddy said grumpily. "Someone obviously tried to kill you. Why would that be?" he asked, eyeballing her.

"I have no idea, or else I guess I would have told you by now, don't you suppose?" Martha was beginning to enjoy the slight tingle the second sip from the flask provided. Teddy reached out, screwed the top on, and placed it back in his inside jacket pocket.

"Are you nosing around Carla Innsbruck's murder?" he asked. Martha said nothing for a moment. She so badly wanted to tell him what she'd seen inside Nick's cabin, but knew he would crash into the place like an elephant in the jungle. There were more threads to this story and she meant to follow them, but *delicately*.

"Of course not," she said to him finally, smiling broadly and shaking her head for good measure. "I've got better things to do with the writing retreat going on." Inside her shoes, she crossed her big and second toes.

"Well, let me drive you girls home. Gail from the ambulance service says you check out fine, but that you'll have a sore couple of days. I'll get the wagon towed to the repair shop and have them give it a once-over."

It was almost six o'clock by the time Teddy finally left. He'd insisted on checking all the doors and windows, as if Mr. Monster Truck had come into the cottage and made himself at home somewhere, and was just waiting to finish Martha off.

After he left, she took a hot shower, downed a few Tylenol, and was sitting on her bed trying to decide what to do next when her cell phone rang. Penny was curled on the bed behind her, sticking close after their frightening afternoon. Martha picked up her phone to find PJ on the line.

"You OK? Chief Perry stopped by to tell us what happened. What in the world, honey? Should we come over? We're getting a little busy with dinner rush, but I could ask Lew to cover. You just tell us what's best."

Martha smiled at PJ's mother hen side coming out. "I'm OK, really. I just needed to shower and put some fresh clothes on. I figure tomorrow I may—"

She was cut off by a loud but muffled sound. She could just make out, "Keep your cargo pants on, Helen... Well, OK, but I was just—"

Suddenly, Helen's voice sounded on the line. "Martha? Are you there?" she asked.

"Yes, I'm here—"

"Good. Now listen. Oh, and I am glad you're OK. That must have been terrifying! But look. You know when you were telling me about Brian Nelson, the ornithology professor and Carla's ex-husband?"

"Yes, I know who you're talking about. But, Helen—"

"Well, after we talked about bird-friendly coffee, you mentioned what he said about his research on bird strikes. And I got curious about that because it's something that came up in the DLT's last board meeting." Helen, Martha knew, served on the board of the Doris Lee Tarberry Nature Center, known to the locals as the DLT. It was made up of land left to Riley Creek by Doris Tarberry in the early 1900s and now served as a birding and wildlife preserve.

Helen continued in an excited tone, "Well, I did some googling and I found something interesting. Nelson is *definitely* significant in the field, so that much is true, but I'm not sure he told you the whole truth. He's also a nominee for the Berringer Award, which is a lifetime achievement award given by his professional organization. I was thinking about it and, well... I don't suppose an association with someone who's just publicly proclaimed herself to be an *anti*-environmentalist can bring much positive PR, can it?"

Martha's wheels were turning. This was a huge development, she felt sure, but she didn't know how it all came together just yet. After all, Nelson wasn't present at the keynote so he couldn't have killed Carla. But as he still benefitted from Carla's death, could he have somehow had something to do with it? She ran her hands through her short hair, tugging.

What I wouldn't give to have Mary Jane here to go through all of these details with me!

Martha thanked Helen and hung up the phone. She didn't have a car since Teddy had made arrangements for hers to be towed to the garage, so whatever her next steps were, they were going to be close to home.

She phoned Margaret, wanting to confirm the next event scheduled for the writers. She knew the schedule by heart, but somehow her brain would not dredge up this evening's details. *Shock*, she said to herself, knowing that traumatic events like car crashes could affect the brain in unpredictable ways.

Margaret answered right away. "Martha, Octavius and I just heard what happened. Are you all right? Can we come over? Is there anything you need?" Martha thought, not for the first time that day, how different a car crash was here than in Boston. She'd been involved in more than one fender-bender in her many years there. Her friends and officemates had shaken their heads, bemoaning Boston drivers, but not much more. Here, she knew that any one of the gals would be at her side if she said the word.

"I'm fine, Margaret, thank you. Hey, do you mind telling me where the writers are right now? Is it free writing time or...?"

"They are scheduled for a wellness break right now, so lots of them are at Ohm Mama with Alexis doing a 'gentle stretching session.'" Martha suspected Margaret was reading this directly from the printed schedule. "Do you need something?"

"No, no, that's OK. I was really hoping to talk to Nick. Have you seen him? Or Liz Waterson?"

"Funny you should ask. I was looking out the front door of Toad in a Hole to see how many were going to take advantage of the wellness break, and I happened to see Liz pop into Looking Sharp. That was probably twenty minutes ago, so she may still be there."

Martha could feel throbbing in her chest and stomach, which she knew was the precursor to days of soreness. She toyed with calling Teddy to tell him about Liz's argument with Carla and the photos she'd seen in Nick's cabin, and forgetting the whole thing.

Why do I have to do all of this snooping?

"By the way, I saw Albert today," Margaret said, as if in answer to Martha's musings. "He said things don't look good for Mary Jane. Apparently, Chief Perry found old news clippings of her marching at pro-environment rallies over the last several years and is suggesting she killed Carla Innsbruck because she was so angry about the keynote."

Martha exploded. "But that makes no sense! Mary Jane has no history of violent behavior, and half of the audience there that night left angry. Why is he singling her out?"

Margaret's voice drew down to almost a whisper. "The fact that she was found leaning over Carla's dead body and Carla was holding her watch in her hand. That might be part of it, but it would just be a guess on my part."

Martha apologized for yelling at Margaret, and they quickly rang off. Then she looked at Penny.

"Girl, I know you want to come along with me, but I need you to stay and rest. You're probably getting as sore as I am." The terrier's silver eyebrows twitched, but her head didn't rise. Martha knew that for once, she wouldn't get an attitude from Penny about being left home alone. She dressed gingerly, beginning to feel new aches from the accident. After popping one more Tylenol for good measure, she headed out the door, determined to get Mary Jane out of Perry's firing line.

Martha was glad she'd thrown a three-quarter zip fleece on before running out the door of the cottage. With the early spring sun dipping down, it was chilly.

The warblers may be returning, but we've got a ways to go till summer, she thought.

She'd only been in Looking Sharp a few times since she tended to frequent Clint's barber shop to get her simple haircuts. Walking in, she expected to be met with the usual scents of a women's hair establishment: a slightly chemical smell with hairspray mixed in. But to Martha's pleasant surprise, the air carried vanilla with hints of something else. Cinnamon, perhaps?

The space was cozy and comfortable. Exposed brick walls held an array of antique Appalachian musical instruments: dulcimers, banjos, and the odd cigar box guitar. A small seating area hosted two comfy, overstuffed leather chairs with a natural wood coffee table that held an assortment of outdoor and home magazines.

There were two stylist chairs, one for hair washing with a giant sink backed onto it, and one that stood upright in front of a mirror. A dryer chair toward the back of the narrow space had an upside-down dome suspended over it. This was where Liz sat reading a book, the sound of the dryer carrying up to the high ceiling.

Using one hand to roll her long braids over her shoulder, Tara Jackson greeted Martha and walked over to her from where she'd been restocking some hair products in the front window. She wore loose-fitting jeans, Birkenstock clogs, and a long-sleeved purple V-neck t-shirt. A waist-length smock was wrapped twice around her middle and tied in front.

"I hope you're not here for a haircut. These writers have just about worn me out. I guess being away from home has made them more inclined to pamper themselves. Or maybe it's these they've come to see." She held her hands out flat for Martha to admire and wiggled all ten fingers. On each of her long orange-painted nails was adhered either a book or a pen.

"Those are fantastic, Tara. But I'm not here for a haircut. I'm actually here to see Liz."

Tara narrowed her eyes and studied Martha for a moment. "Ah," she said. "I see what you're up to. I heard from Alexis that you were doing your *Cagney and Lacey* routine again."

Alexis? What does Alexis know... actually, why does EVERY-ONE know my business? Am I not looking into the murder on the down-low?

"Look, Martha. I know you're trying to help Mary Jane and all, but I don't want any trouble in here. People come here to relax and unwind, maybe spend an hour on themselves, and I don't want you messing that up. See that?" Here, Tara pointed a finger over her shoulder at a sign above the door that read *Namaste. Period.* "That's my motto and that's what goes on in here. There's a reason I'm next to a yoga studio. So if you've got to talk to Liz, talk, but the minute she looks less than Zenful, I'm kicking you out."

Martha gave her most innocent smile, nodded her thanks and understanding, then walked as casually as she could the twenty paces to where Liz sat. She waved a hand at Liz, who pushed the dryer dome up a few inches so she could hear.

"Liz, I'm sorry to bother you, but I need to ask you a few questions if that's OK?" Martha said, trying for Southern breezy, but sounding stilted, even to her own ears.

"*Okayyyy...*" Liz replied, the end of her sentence going up an octave to reflect her confusion.

"You told me that you had no personal relationship to Carla. I've been told otherwise and I was just wondering if you wouldn't mind explaining a bit more?" This sweet stuff was for the birds, but Martha didn't dare ask Liz her questions as directly as she wanted to. Tara would kick her out faster than she could say "Please don't kick me out!"

"Otherwise? Can you be more specific?" Liz said. There was the resting B face.

"Well, someone told me they saw you and Carla arguing on the front porch of your house last week. I was just curious why you didn't tell me about that. Why were you arguing?" Martha asked with mild curiosity, in spite of the darkening look on Liz Waterson's face. Martha could feel Tara's eyes boring into her back and she tried to line up her body with Liz's expression to keep Tara from seeing.

"I'm not sure I see how it's any of your business, but I have no problem telling you. I didn't mention it because, well, it's still true what I said. I had no relationship to her. Until last week, I'd never met her in my life. Then, one day, she comes marching up my driveway, ranting about me removing trees to make way for my 'Hummer house,' as she called it. I tried to explain to her that it was LEED certified, but she didn't want to hear it."

Martha heard Tara take a few steps across the creaky wooden floor, drawing nearer, and turned to her with a big smile, indicating they were just having a friendly chat.

"Then she started talking about the 'land deal' out by the DLT and how she knew all about my 'dirty little secret,'" Liz continued. "I told her it was no secret, that I was just one small investor in a whole group supporting the new nature center near the state park. Check it out yourself. It's a group my brother-in-law put together. Mockingbird Limited is the name of the company."

Martha's brain was working in overdrive, but not very successfully. Why would Carla have been so upset about a nature center? In fact, hadn't she suddenly become *pro*-development, based on her keynote remarks?

"I think she had too many bats in her belfry, if you ask me," Liz said. By this time, Tara was looming over Martha's shoulder.

"Time to go, Cagney," her deep voice boomed.

"Right. Yeah. Namaste," Martha replied, giving a short wave to both women as she stood up and headed out the front door.

New Canaan, Tennessee, United States, April 6, 1892

I AM HAPPY TO REPORT that Double Oaks has been completed! Just last week, our fellow farmers helped us to raise the last structure, a small barn for our herd of beef cattle. It is just a start, but means the world to Thomas, Susannah, and me. We have plans to expand to sheep and pigs, hopefully in a year from now.

Susannah and I have become betrothed, and over time Thomas has accepted it, albeit grudgingly. That is not to say that these past months have not seen many harsh words and painful conversations, some overheard through our adjoining walls as I paced the floor of my half of Double Oaks. But blessedly, Thomas has come to tolerate—dare I say accept?—our relationship. He and I leave early each morning to tend to the animals and care for our expanding fields, and some of our old camaraderie is back.

Other news to report: Mother is coming to New Canaan to visit! While the train spur is still uncertain, it has been nearly two years since we parted, and because I cannot leave the farm just now, she has decided to come to me. Alas, Cyril will not be joining her, for much the same reason as I, though in his case his burden is one of land oversight, not plowing and planting with his own hands as I do. I cannot wait to show Mother our home, fields, livestock, and all around New Canaan.

In a strange twist of fate, my newfound investment in the land has brought my brother and me closer than ever. Of course, only in our letters to one another, but we finally have a truly shared interest. As they say, absence does make the heart grow fonder, but it also allows one to see things from an angle not possible when the other is too close at hand. So it is with my brother and me.

Our small community continues, yet its growth has slowed considerably with the destruction of the inn and ongoing uncertainty about the rail line's arrival. Thomas and I are hopeful as that connection to nearby cities will be critical to our farm's success and eventual growth. Surely investors in Boston and at the railway company will come to their senses soon.

Chapter Twelve

Martha blew out the front door of Looking Sharp and almost bumped right into Alexis Bloom as she left the yoga studio. "Hey, Martha!" Alexis said lightly, her cheeks flushed pink. "I was just going to grab a coffee from PJ, then pop back upstairs to shower. I'm joining some of the writers for dinner in Adair. There's a new nose-to-tail place they want to check out and I figured, why not? You want to come?"

Not sure she was in the mood to consume either a nose or a tail, Martha declined and walked across the square to Silent Sisters. She hadn't talked to Ethel Jean since the older woman had all but thrown her out and she knew a check-in was overdue. She pushed on the door to the sound of a tinkling bell.

Ethel Jean was nowhere in sight. "Hello?" Martha called.

"In here," came a gruff response. Martha made her way past tasteful arrangements of antique silverware, lamps, and books with fine-tooled leather spines to the space in the rear of the shop. Aunt Lorna and Mary Jane had reconfigured this space to become a classroom where various courses were taught, most of them for birders during the height of the spring migration season. The height of the season that would be here in just a few weeks, Martha reflected anxiously.

Surely Mary Jane will be free by then?

She found Ethel Jean and Margaret huddled with a pile of manila files, Margaret tapping the keys on a large adding machine that was spitting out inches of paper tape. She looked up at Martha with a pleading expression in her eyes.

"Whadda you want?" Ethel Jean sneered at Martha. "I thought I told you to get out there and figure out who killed that woman so we can get my sister out of jail before your boyfriend railroads her."

"Ethel Jean, I've been gathering information all weekend. I was just coming in to check on you and see how you were holding up."

"My sister is in jail, that's how I'm holding up." Martha had drawn close enough that she could now see how exhausted the older woman looked.

Quietly, Margaret said, "Tell her about Frank's visit."

"Oh yeah," Ethel Jean said, nodding. "My sister's doe-eyed beau went over to see her, took her a chocolate croissant, and she said she didn't want it."

Whoa. Things were going downhill fast.

"She's convinced they are going to send her to prison—big city prison—if not try for the death penalty."

"*WHAT?*" Martha almost yelled.

"Yeah. Apparently, the district attorney in charge of our little backwater is as interested in climbing the ladder as your moronic hunk of love. Between the two of them, they're going to sign, seal and deliver Mary Jane while you're sitting around eating bonbons." As the word escaped her, Ethel Jean's eyes teared up. Martha knew why. They all knew why. Mary Jane *loved* bonbons. Would she ever again get to enjoy them?

"Now, you get out of here and get busy solving this thing," Ethel Jean said.

Feeling as rebuffed as she'd been at Looking Sharp, Martha headed to her cottage, shaking off sympathetic offers from PJ and Helen to join her and watch over her for the evening. She trudged home, the fiery sunset adding insult to injury. How could she enjoy a single ray of the sun—even less this glorious display—while one of her best friends sat in jail because of an event that *she* had organized?

"Martha?" came Delores's voice just as Martha had been about to let herself in through the little picket fence gate in front of her cottage. She'd had her head down and had been so completely lost in her own thoughts that she hadn't even seen Delores out in her front yard. She'd been gardening and still had gloves on and a trowel in her hand.

Delores headed across the road and stood close to Martha. "Child, you have hardly been home for three days. Are you all right?" She peered at Martha, and then said, "No, clearly you are not all right."

Martha gave her the short version of what had been a very long day. She saw Delores's brow furrow deeply once she filled her in on the truck running her off the road.

Delores glanced down at her smartwatch. "It's almost dinnertime and Jimmy is making pasta Bolognese. Why don't you join us? You don't have to stay, but you *do* have to eat. I won't take no for an answer. The children can play in the garden."

Martha took a deep breath and agreed to freshen up and come on over. She'd just sit and stew anyway, and she couldn't remember the last time she'd eaten. She opened the door, letting Penny run over to Delores. A few minutes later, Martha was knocking on the Ritzenwallers' front door.

Entering, she took in an aroma that nearly made her weak in the knees. She knew there was homemade Bolognese on the stove top, but what was that other smell? Ahhh... garlic rolls. Jimmy had shared his homemade garlic rolls on another occasion, and they were heavenly.

Jimmy emerged from the kitchen in pressed jeans and a light flannel shirt with the sleeves rolled up. He handed Martha and Delores a glass of wine each with just a single word: "Malbec." Delores gave Jimmy the bare-bones story of the truck running Martha off the road. Jimmy was silent, but his cheeks flushed before he turned back to the kitchen.

Delores and Martha made small talk about the nature writers' retreat, but Martha's mind kept trawling through the various threads she'd gathered over the past couple of days. So, when Jimmy came out of the kitchen with his glass of wine and sat, she was relieved that he had a question.

"Where are things with your investigation?"

Martha was too exhausted to protest his choice of words, and simply said, "It's a mess. There are so many possibilities, and I just can't make heads or tails of them."

"And what would you normally do in such a case?" he asked gently.

"Well, that's the thing. Normally, I would go over everything with Mary Jane. Not that she's particularly objective, but she *does* let me bounce ideas and perspectives around."

Jimmy looked at his wife. "Well, we're not Mary Jane, but why don't we give it a try?"

"No, no," Martha objected. "We're about to eat."

"Nonsense," Delores said, setting her wine down on a coaster and getting up. "We can eat in the kitchen and talk things through at the same time. It will be more interesting than most dinners we have, I can assure you." Jimmy raised his eyebrows at his wife, and she met his gaze and sent him an air kiss as she pushed through the swinging kitchen door with her backside.

In moments, the three of them were seated around the kitchen island on wooden bar stools with padded backs, Jimmy having brought Delores's glass in as well as his own. Delores had pulled out a giant paper easel and markers from a closet, explaining that Jimmy sometimes used them to sketch woodworking projects. Jimmy put pasta and salad down in front of everyone, topped up their wine, and they commenced.

"Mary Jane and I usually start with the most obvious suspects. In this case, that's actually Mary Jane herself," Martha said, taking a too-large bite of a garlic roll. Delores, who was sitting next to the easel, wrote Mary Jane's name at the top of the paper.

"So, what makes Mary Jane a suspect, besides being discovered over Carla Innsbruck's body?" Jimmy asked.

Martha counted on her fingers. "One, she was over the body. Two, she had blood on her hands. Three, Carla had Mary Jane's watch clutched in her hand."

"Well, I heard that Mary Jane already explained the watch. Carla had asked to borrow it so she wouldn't go over her allotted time during the keynote." Delores looked pleased, and Martha contemplated again how this couple, far from being busybodies like Angie Bangor, somehow managed to be in the know.

Martha held up another finger. "And four, Mary Jane's love of all things environmental may have caused her to lose her mind at Carla's remarks and kill her on the spot."

"*Pfft*," Jimmy said, taking a long sip of the deep and spicy Malbec.

"I know, I know. But we have to be as objective as we can and look at every possibility."

"Who's next?" asked Delores, capping the marker she'd been using for a moment and bending over for a bite of salad.

"Let's go with Ivan Gregory, Carla's editor. He was in the audience for the keynote, as was Sherry. She was Carla's 'handler' from the publishing company, so to speak. Ivan told me himself that he was angry about an overdue manuscript for an autobiography that Carla had promised him. Sherry could have been angry for the same reason."

"I hate to state the obvious, but killing her would definitely *not* have helped get the manuscript delivered," Jimmy said.

"Yes, but do you remember what we learned in winter, Martha?" Delores interjected. "That book sales, especially for biographies and autobiographies, tend to increase when the subject is deceased?"

Martha gave a quick shiver. "Yes, good point. We should jot that down."

Delores squeaked the marker along the easel page.

"Who else?" Jimmy prompted.

"Well, there is an ex-husband. Brian Nelson," Martha said. "He admitted that Carla was very difficult and could make him crazy. But he's remarried now and I can't imagine him risking that much over old wounds. However..."

Delores and Jimmy looked at her, waiting for her to say more.

"Well, Helen did some digging and it seems Brian is up for a prestigious award, one where one's chances might be dashed due to any association with controversy."

Jimmy picked up the thread. "As in, the kind of controversy that might come from a famous environmentalist suddenly proclaiming that it is time to let the Earth kill itself to bring in a new era?"

"Yes, as an example, that kind of controversy. But the one thing about Nelson is that he was not in attendance at the keynote."

"Could he have hired someone to bump her off?" Delores said, getting into the spirit of things. She refilled wine glasses as Martha and Jimmy stared at her. "What?" she asked.

"Yes, he could have, so I guess we keep him on the list," Martha agreed.

Jimmy pointed at the easel with his fork. "What about the people who were in the church at the time she was found?"

"Well, if you agree that the murderer couldn't be me, Octavius, Helen or Margaret, that leaves a handful of people because most, including Sherry and Ivan, left straight after the keynote. We saw them leave with our own eyes. All the writers gathered to review the agenda, and the only ones who stayed behind after that were Nick, Karen, Angie, and Liz."

"Liz Waterson, the lady who moved back a bit ago and wrote the piece about Carla in the paper?" Delores asked.

Martha nodded. "Yes, she wrote that piece, and yes, she's recently moved back and built a big house out on Rhubarb Pike. I've spoken to her and one thing is odd. At first, she said she had no relationship to Carla, but I've since found out Carla came to her house and the two of them got into a tiff. First about the trees Liz removed to build the house, and second about a piece of land near the state park. The Mockingbird Limited project. Do you know anything about that?"

"Just what everyone knows," Jimmy answered. "It's going to be some kind of nature center."

"Liz admitted to being one of the investors, but apparently Carla was really upset about it. Sherry also said she'd been going out to that area a lot lately instead of attending to her manuscript."

"That is odd indeed," Delores said.

"Anyway, the two argued, but Liz seemed to have a perfectly plausible explanation for it."

"But that makes Carla sound like she was still truly an environmentalist at heart. Then a few days later, she goes off the deep end in her keynote remarks," Jimmy said. "That doesn't fit."

"How about the other three?" Delores asked. She'd finished her dinner now and stood sentinel at the easel, marker in hand. Flipping the page with a flourish, she wrote the other three writers' names down.

"Let's start with Karen," said Martha. "She's from Johnson City, Tennessee and works as an editor. Seems nice enough." *As Aunt Lorna used to say, everyone has at least one redeeming quality.*

"Actually, I have something about her," Delores said with a hint of what sounded like pride. "I was walking back from the library late afternoon today and Margaret came running out of the bookshop. She said she probably wouldn't see you, but she asked me to tell you something if I did." Delores paused a moment and looked skyward, working hard to dredge something from her memory. "She said to tell you that Karen had been rejected by Carla. She'd sent her a piece of writing and asked her opinion of it, and Carla tore it to pieces. Yes, that's what Margaret said. She said Karen mentioned that in their small critique group."

"That's an interesting twist. She hasn't mentioned that to me. Don't suppose it's enough to make her murder Carla, but let's note it down."

Delores wrote.

"Who does that leave us with?" Jimmy asked.

"Nick and Angie," said Martha. "Angie is probably thirty-something I'd guess, an admin assistant in Nashville, contemplating a master's in fine arts, and as far as I can tell, she has absolutely no connection to Carla. The only other thing that's notable about her is that she's a bit of a gossip, for whatever it's worth. Now Nick..." she trailed off.

"What about him?" Jimmy asked. Martha had to tread carefully here. If she told the Ritzenwallers what she'd seen in his cabin, they'd likely (*and perhaps rightly*, she thought) insist on calling the police. She still wasn't ready to do that and take the chance of Teddy finding out she'd been snooping around.

"Nick is a professional photographer by trade. Kind of a big mouth, in my opinion, very self-assured," Martha remarked.

"What's he doing at a writers' retreat?" Delores asked.

"You know, I'm not totally sure about that. Why don't I make it a point to fall into conversation with him tomorrow and see if I can find out more?"

"Carefully, and in a room full of people," Jimmy warned her. Martha grinned.

"Yes, Dad."

They all studied the notes Delores had written on the easel. Jimmy cleared the dishes, then poured coffee from a thermos for all of them and served each a delectable-looking slice of chocolate tart.

"Will you keep feeding me if I can come up with more suspects?" Martha asked, laughing. The wine and food had relaxed her, and she'd needed this chance to organize the information she'd gathered more than she had realized.

"To be honest, the people who seem to have the strongest motives are the editor, Ivan, and the handler, as you called her. Sherry. They were counting on the manuscript to produce a bestseller," Delores said, putting her chin in her hand and leaning her elbow on top of the island. "But if I'm Teddy, thinking Mary Jane, found over the victim who's holding her watch, is the most likely suspect I've got in terms of physical evidence, I'm not sure I see an enraged murderer coming through from the rest of these notes."

"I'm afraid I have to agree, and that doesn't help Mary Jane. I must be missing something, and I've got to work out what that is," Martha said, forking up her tart.

"But that means Chief Perry is probably also missing something," Jimmy said casually.

"You're assuming he's still not looking anywhere but at Mary Jane," Martha said, easing her dessert plate down into the farmhouse sink. She thanked Jimmy and Delores, and then scooped Penny up from the front porch where she and Fritz had been lolling. Martha guessed from the little dog's dead weight in her arms that the two had run all over the yard to the point of exhaustion.

She got home and saw that she'd missed multiple calls from Teddy. She texted him that she was fine, thanked him for his help with her station wagon, and told him goodnight. Then she took a hot shower, and joined Penny in her twin bed. Would she ever move out of her childhood space and into Lorna's big room? That was not something to contemplate tonight, while Mary Jane was probably lying on a metal bunk.

Nick was her missing piece, Martha was sure. She lay pondering the best way to confront him about his photos of Carla Innsbruck. Somewhere during her plotting and scheming, she drifted away to sleep.

New Canaan, Tennessee, United States, August 12, 1892

MOTHER IS HERE! HAVING not seen her for two full years, I was overjoyed when her carriage arrived from Boston.

She is quite a bit aged from when I saw her last, but she tells me I am changed as well. I laughed when she reached out to feel my bicep, because as small boys, Cyril and I would often ask her to do this and pick the son whose muscles were larger.

I let her rest overnight. The following day, Thomas, Susannah and I took her in Mr. Peterson's buggy to see all of New Canaan: our fields, the church, the library, the many homesteads, and the mercantile. The old inn's tennis court is still very much in use and she exclaimed at the sight of the burnt-out shell that served as its backdrop. We have gotten used to it, but I suppose the sight of the inn's charred remains just beyond the court is a bit unsettling to newcomers.

I am embarrassed to admit in these pages that I'd been a bit unsure of how Mother would respond to Thomas and Susannah. She knew of them from my letters, but she was also raised in a monied family. I expected her to be not unfriendly, but perhaps... aloof. To the contrary, she allows Thomas to slip her arm through his as we explore the various sights and, much to my surprise, agreed when he suggested a picnic for tomorrow. He promised her he will help her to find a comfortable seat upon one of the giant boulders that line our river.

Mother has told me that Susannah is "a great beauty" and more intelligent than most of the privately educated girls she knows in London who have made their formal debuts. My chest swells with pride to see them talk and laugh over private jokes. How I have missed Mother.

Tonight, she dines with Mr. Hicks and his family. Thomas has been feeling poorly and Susannah will remain with him for a quiet evening at home, so I have had the opportunity to make these entries. What happy days!

Chapter Thirteen

Martha could hardly believe it was already Sunday. She sat on her back deck with a cup of perfectly creamed Birder Blend, watching Penny scour Bird Paradise for any breaking news.

Tonight was the closing ceremony for the retreat, and Martha felt guilty that she'd been so uninvolved in the writers' events. True, it sounded like they had frequented local businesses, but she hoped her friends and fellow retailers didn't feel she'd heaved off the hard work on them while she nosed around.

Once her coffee was drained and Penny had come back, they went inside where Martha showered and got ready for the day. She knew a friend of Don's was doing an Intro to Trout Fishing workshop this morning, after which the writers had free time to finalize any writing or other last tasks they wanted to accomplish. The closing ceremony, which had been planned to take place in the church, had been moved to the Tarberry House on the grounds of the DLT. The quaint building had been home to Doris Tarberry's family and was now used for intimate gatherings such as business retreats, class reunions, and the like. It was perfect.

Martha was getting ready to head for the shop with Penny when her phone rang. She saw from the screen that it was Allison. She swiped to take the call and wedged the phone between her cheek and shoulder as she locked the front door.

"Hey, Allison, how are you? What's happening?"

"*Bonjour, mon amie*! *C'est Joanne.* Allison asked me to call you while she and Noah are in McDonald's. We are on our way home. *Finally.*"

"Finally? You've only been gone a day or two."

"Martha, let me tell you, a day or two with Monsieur Noah feels like an eternity."

"That bad?"

"*Oui.*"

"But did Allison get everything straightened out in Memphis?" Martha asked as she came around the corner and into the square.

"*Oui.* Apparently being a policewoman helps a great deal in such situations. She has temporary custody of the boy and we're bringing him back to Riley Creek. From there... it's hard to say."

"I'm sure he's upset, having lost his mom and so on," Martha said.

"Yes, and perhaps that is part of his trouble. But he is... difficult. Anyway, she wanted me to let you know we are on our way. Has the Chief released Mary Jane? I've called Ethel Jean a few times to check in, but she's stopped taking my calls. Says I'm hovering, if you can believe that! She said something about blocking me, and now when I call, it rings one time and goes directly to voicemail." Here, Joanne said something else in French that Martha didn't recognize, but guessed it was not something she'd want to translate in mixed company.

"Well, you know Ethel Jean. Deep down, she appreciates that you care, but has a hard time showing it. Look, Joanne, I'd love to keep talking, but I'm super busy. Mary Jane is still in jail and the retreat closing ceremony is tonight. I've got a few leads to follow and I've got to help get things ready for this evening."

They rang off with Joanne telling Martha she and Allison would arrive back in Riley Creek that evening unless something happened with the "little darling." Somehow, Martha didn't think it was a term of endearment.

She opened the shop door, unclipped Penny and took in the sharp scent of roasting. PJ was behind the counter, filling urns for the self-serve area.

"Did you roast last night? Why didn't you tell me? I would have helped."

PJ nodded toward the back window, through which Martha could see Helen refilling feeders. "Helen helped me. We knew you were too tired from all of your running around. We've got the new beans arriving soon—the bird-friendly ones—so wanted to go ahead and roast and package up the rest of what we had in stock. Would you believe we've already had two writers come in to buy coffee for home?"

Looking over to the display rack, Martha took in the healthy stock of coffee by the pound.

"Well, thanks. I'm hoping once the retreat wraps up, we can get back to normal a bit..." she trailed off, neither of them acknowledging that normal would never come unless Mary Jane was with them.

Helen came in the back door and walked straight over to Martha.

"Hey, Martha. Nick was in here this morning. You missed him by five minutes. Margaret"—here, she nodded at Margaret, who was hard at work at her own laptop, but now glanced over at them and waved—"overheard him talking about skipping the trout fishing workshop and taking a last hike. When he paid his bill, I made a point of recommending the Hungry Honey trail."

"Ah. Let me guess," Martha said. "One of you talked to Delores this morning?"

"Last night," PJ said casually, rubbing down the counter as if it were the fender chrome on a Mustang GT.

Margaret crept over to join them.

"Margaret, I'm surprised you've joined in with Gossip Girls here."

She had the decency to blush, but then said, "Actually, I wanted to tell you something, Martha."

"Oh, Delores gave me your message about Karen last night, how Carla had torn up some of her writing once upon a time."

Margaret nodded. "Well, yes, there was that. But also, I'm not actually sure Nick is a writer. That is to say, he was in our critique group yesterday, but I don't think he's actually written anything while he's been here."

"Maybe he was too intimidated as a new writer to share anything?"

"Maybe, but he didn't even seem interested, and didn't offer any critiques of anyone else's writing either. He mostly typed on his phone."

Martha took this in before she turned to Helen and PJ.

"As much as I don't like gossiping, just this once, thanks to all three of you for the useful information. Do you girls think you can hold down the fort for a bit? I know we've got to get things ready for tonight, and since it seems I'll now be heading toward the DLT, can I take anything over?"

PJ brushed her off. "No, no. Nothing. And we are definitely good to hold down the fort. Tonight is mainly desserts, and Cat and Carl have got that all covered. We'll bring the coffee."

"Oh, sure," came Ethel Jean's voice from the hallway connecting the shop to Silent Sisters. "Let Charlie's Angel just trot off, getting out of work as usual."

Martha gave PJ and Helen each a hard look. "Go," they said, almost in unison. PJ reached under the counter and came up with Martha's set of car keys.

"You might need these. Teddy dropped it off in the back lot last night. I think he knows you aren't really all that enthusiastic about seeing him right now."

Martha snatched up the keys and flew out the back door as PJ picked up her phone to tap in a number.

Martha knew Penny, who'd gone straight up to the shop's office and her lambswool dog bed, would be none too happy when she found out her human had headed out for a hike without her. But this was less of a hike and more of a mission, and Martha needed all of the focus she could muster.

She parked at the cottage, ran in and changed her shoes, grabbed her pack and some basics, and jumped back in her wagon to head out to the DLT. She knew without asking why Helen had suggested the Hungry Honey. It was an out and back trail, which meant that if Nick was on it, Martha would be sure to run into him. It was also a trail that was out in the open and ran along the river, popular with dog walkers and hikers alike. In other words, the chances of Nick shivving her right there were relatively thin.

Martha pulled into the parking lot and saw Jimmy sitting in his Land Rover in the spot closest to the trailhead. She shouldered her pack and walked over to his open driver's side window.

"What is it with you guys? Let me see: it's *you* PJ called as soon as I left the shop?"

"Could be," Jimmy said. "Here. Take this." He handed her a walkie-talkie. "Delores and I bought these after using Jason's last winter. She likes to call me on hers when she's in the yard and needs me to come out and help her with something."

Martha remembered well how useful the walkie-talkies had been during the winter blizzard.

"OK. Got it."

"Keep it on. I don't think anyone would try anything out here"—Jimmy gestured at the few other hikers milling around in the parking lot—"but I may mosey up the trail just in case."

She pushed the walkie-talkie into the side pocket of her pack, then turned to go. Over her shoulder, she waved a hand and called back to him.

"Thanks, Dad. I'll be fine."

Martha headed up the trail, grateful for its lack of incline so that she could make good time. Within five minutes, she'd hit a regular stride, but she still felt her heart pounding.

I've got to do a better job of prioritizing exercise. As soon as this is over and I've figured out who really killed Carla.

She overtook all but the trail runners who called out "passing on your left" from behind before they zoomed by. The trail was two and a half miles out and back, but she didn't spot Nick until about a mile in. She recognized his ponytail right away. He wasn't wearing a pack and had on a pair of worn Nikes.

She sped up, came alongside him, and then said, "Oh, hey, Nick! Fancy meeting you out here. I figured you'd be at the fly fishing workshop this morning. I was just getting in a hike before the evening's festivities." Martha was impressed at her own breeziness. *How have I learned to fib so well?*

"Uh, oh, hey, Martha. Yeah, fishing isn't for me. I thought I'd do a hike before heading back to... finish some last writing."

This guy needs to work on his lying, she thought.

Now they were walking in tandem, Martha on his left. "Mind if I come along with you for a bit?" she asked.

"Um, sure, no problem," Nick replied grudgingly.

"I'm not sure if I heard how you got into writing," Martha said, continuing her Southern breezy routine.

"Well, it's a long story," Nick said, waving his hand dismissively.

"Oh, that's OK. I love long stories on a sunny day."

Nick pushed out a long breath. "Well, let's say I want to explore the 'journalism' side of photojournalism," he said flatly.

"But I'm guessing you aren't totally done with photography," Martha said, reaching back with her left hand to pull out the walkie-talkie in one fluid motion. She held it in her hand, her thumb hovering over what she always called the "talkie" button.

Nick glanced sideways at her, but returned his eyes quickly to the ground ahead of him. "Why do you say that?" he asked.

"Well, I was near the cabins the other day, doing a little wild-flower hike, and I popped over to see if anyone was around. No one was, but I couldn't help noticing the impressive collection of photos hanging up in yours." She kept her voice cheerful, as if displaying pictures of a woman who'd just been murdered was the most normal thing in the world.

"You had no right to invade my privacy like that!" he said, stopping and looking her straight in the eye.

She held up the walkie-talkie and gestured with a smile to some hikers that were approaching from about fifty yards away. "My friend at the other end of this walkie-talkie will call 911 the minute

I say 'boo' and I am sure you wouldn't want to try anything in front of all of these nice people."

As the hikers neared, Nick and Martha eased off of the trail to make room.

"Hi, y'all! Awesome day for a hike," Martha called sweetly. As soon as the hikers passed, she resumed a completely serious face.

"Nick, you need to tell it to me straight or so help me, my friend is going to call the Riley Creek PD and fill them in on those photos." She waggled the walkie-talkie back and forth to add emphasis.

"It's not what you think," he said, all swagger gone now.

"What I think is that you followed Carla Innsbruck and murdered her."

"No, no! That's not how it went at all! You've got to believe me!" Nick's ponytail snapped side to side as he shook his head in the negative.

"Let's go over to those rocks and talk," Martha said, pointing to some large boulders along the river. She made Nick go first. She didn't think he was going to try anything, but she wasn't in the mood for a chase.

They clambered up a large boulder that overlooked the river.

"You'd better come clean and quick. My friend is in jail for someone else's actions and I'm losing patience. Fast. Now spill it." Martha was impressed at how easily she'd shifted from breezy to tough. *I'm getting pretty good at this stuff,* she thought.

"All right, all right. But I have a question first. I may have... lied to the police. If I tell you, are you going to tell them?" He bit his lip as he waited for Martha to answer.

"Let's not worry about that right now. I may be able to put in a good word for you, depending on what you tell me and if it helps us get to the real killer." What she didn't say was that she suspect-ed her "pull" with the police to plummet drastically once a certain Chief found out she had in fact been nosing around.

Nick seemed to think this over, and finally started talking. "I was paid for the photos," he said.

"By whom? Why?"

"I'm not exactly sure who, except that the guy that came for the photos drove a huge monster truck."

"Black? With a rhino bar on the front?" Martha asked anxious-ly.

"Yes. How did you know?"

"Never mind that. How did you find him?"

"I didn't find him. He found me. He somehow knew I had... *history* with Carla Innsbruck, and called to see if I'd like to pay her back, and get paid some cash on top of it. All I had to do was spend a week or so following her, attend this workshop and pretend to be a writer, then go home. Easiest money I'd ever make, I figured, so I jumped at it."

"How did you and Monster Truck connect?"

"We set up a time and place to meet, and the week before the retreat, he put me up in a hotel a few miles from Innsbruck's house. I followed her the few times she left the house, mainly for groceries and to hike around a spot in the woods a ways beyond the state park. Then I met him at the appointed time and gave him the pho-tos."

"So those were copies you hung up?"

"Yes. I always keep copies from any paid job. After she was killed at the church, I wanted to see if there was anything in the photos that could help the police. I really didn't think there was, so

I didn't tell them. I can't afford any trouble and I'm pretty sure I'd have plenty of it if I crossed Monster Truck."

"I'm going to need those photos," Martha said. Nick nodded. "I guess there's something I don't understand. Why would Monster Truck have contacted you in the first place? What history do you have with Carla?"

Nick dropped his head down, pulled his hair out of its ponytail, and ran a hand through it. "She got me in huge trouble with my employer a few years back. See, I'd had an assignment to do a shoot of a national park out west for a magazine. They paid me up front, and then I got invited to a long weekend with friends in New York City the same time that I'd planned to travel and do the shoot. It was just a small magazine, so I decided to improvise and recycle photos from other shoots so that I could still make the New York trip. The magazine accepted them and didn't know the difference. Apparently, Carla Innsbruck saw the piece and contacted them right away. Something about the birds in the photo being *eastern* bluebirds and the white pines being *eastern* pines. I don't know."

He waved a dismissive hand before continuing. "Anyway, the magazine demanded its money back and printed a big retraction in its next issue, and it's been hard for me to find work ever since. So when this Mockingbird company or whatever contacted me and asked if I'd like to return the favor, I jumped on the chance to do anything that would get Innsbruck in trouble."

Martha sat up at attention. "Wait a minute. Mockingbird company? But I thought you said you didn't know who paid you for the photos."

Nick looked up at the sky for a minute. "You know, I guess when you asked me, I didn't think about it. But on the electronic money transfer, that's what showed up. Hang on." He tapped a few words into his phone, then held the screen up for Martha to see. Nick was right. *Mockingbird LLC* followed by a long series of numbers appeared next to the date of the money transfer.

"Is there anything else you haven't told me? Or haven't told the police?" Martha asked.

"Only that I had nothing to do with Innsbruck getting murdered. As soon as she did, I figured Monster Truck was involved and that meant I was involved too. I've just been counting down the days till I can get out of here and back to the city. I don't want anything to do with any of this." His wide eyes reminded Martha of Penny's the moment they were called into the veterinarian's exam room.

She grasped Nick's upper arm gently. "I need you to get me those photos. Provided everything you've told me is true, you're not going to be charged with Carla's murder. But someone else sure is."

New Canaan, Tennessee, United States, October 10 or 11, 1892

AS I COMMIT THESE WORDS to these pages, I'm not even certain of the date. I only know it has been days since any of us has slept, and my mind begins to play tricks on me.

Thomas was one of the earliest in our community to contract typhoid. He died almost four weeks to the day after he began showing symptoms. I will not repeat here the agony he endured. I tried to spare his sister the worst of it, and insisted Thomas remain with me while I did my best to minister to him. Alas, my meager skills were no match for this cruel disease, and we lost him.

Since my last writing, we have lost so many, the most acutely felt being Thomas, of course, but also Mrs. Peterson and two of her youngest. Susannah, Mother and I live in fear that one of us might begin experiencing the high fever, stomach pain, and diarrhea that have attacked so many of our friends.

When I last saw Pastor Taylor, he looked as haggard and worn as I felt. He said he'd counted twenty-seven souls lost, but feared there might be others, particularly among his elderly congregants, who live far from the village center. It is all he can do to minister to his flock without becoming infected himself. I wonder how long it will be before we lose him from illness or simple exhaustion.

Two months ago, the young men and women of the upper classes, who had never been particularly suited to a life of toil and could not grow accustomed to the hard work that being in this community requires, began leaving. Thanks to their inability to plan crops accordingly, we were already going to face a difficult winter. Now that they have left and we have lost so many able-bodied men, we almost surely face a treacherous time. Of the sixty or so families that Mr. Hicks started with, fewer than twenty of us remain.

The morning I traveled to Mr. Hicks to give him the news of Thomas's death, he delivered another blow. The rail spur would not be coming to New Canaan. I have no doubt giving me this news pained him greatly; he had tears in his eyes as he shared it. He explained that the rail company had long been skeptical about our community's ability to grow and provide a profitable route, and our recent losses convinced them of its impossibility.

This news was almost more than I could take. I am ashamed to say that I remained away from Double Oaks for several hours as I struggled to come to terms with it.

Yet with all of this bleak news, all of this loss, comes a ray of hope: Susannah suspects she is with child. She told me only days after we'd lost Thomas. We asked Pastor Taylor to unite us, explaining to him and Mother only that Thomas's death made us realize the fleeting nature of life and we wanted to be married as soon as possible. It was not the ceremony either of us had dreamed of when we'd planned it in words so many times, but truly, it was perfect. Only Pastor Taylor and Mother were there as our witnesses. Our vows were heartfelt and I cannot help but be overjoyed at the notion that a child may be joining us in the coming months.

We three—Mother, Susannah and I—now share one side of the duplex, making chores, meals and heating more efficient. Susannah has begun to feel ill in the early mornings, not due to typhoid as we first feared, but from the demands of the baby she believes is growing inside of her. Mother and I have quietly discussed going home to England. Cyril continues to do well and, truthfully, life would be easier there, particularly for Mother who has been such a strength to Su-

sannah and me these last months. But, truthfully, I find I am not yet ready to end my time here. And Susannah cannot even talk about a coach journey to Boston. She has already told me a ship voyage is beyond contemplation in her current condition.

Mr. Hicks has asked for a meeting of the remaining New Canaan men. I will open the library and clean it. It has been out of use these many weeks of illness, but remains the warmest place for a small group to meet once one sets its fireplace to burning. I do not know what will come of this meeting, but of course, I fear Mr. Hicks will announce the end of our great experiment.

Chapter Fourteen

When Nick and Martha emerged back at the trailhead, she walked behind him and gave Jimmy an OK sign with her thumb and index finger. She then got into her Subaru and followed Nick back to his cabin, waiting while he gathered up all the photos for her.

Martha still wasn't sure how the pieces fit together, but she knew she was onto something with Mockingbird LLC. Liz was connected to it somehow, by her own admission, and the company had had Nick follow Carla. Then Carla ended up dead. Liz was looking more and more likely as the killer, but what could Martha do to strengthen her theory and present it all to Teddy so that he would let Mary Jane go and pursue the *real* murderer?

Martha parked behind the shop and headed in. She felt a bit warm and fanned herself with the photos in her hand as she opened the back door. Was spring about to flip right on into summer? Riley Creekers always raved about the nice long springs they enjoyed.

After the terrible winter storm, we are due that much, darn it! Martha thought.

As she stepped in, Octavius, Margaret, PJ and Helen all jumped away from the counter where they'd been clustered around PJ's laptop. They looked like four guilty dogs who had just pulled the Thanksgiving turkey off the counter, eaten it, and were now looking sideways at one another.

"OK, you four. What are you up to?" Martha asked.

"It's pretty amazing, actually," PJ said, clicking the track pad with her finger. "We've added some pictures of Penny"—here, she turned the laptop so Martha could see—"and people are going wild!"

Martha leaned in to see Penny sleeping in her bed; Penny watching the birds out the back window; Penny in the office chair, looking at the computer screen with a pair of readers balanced on her snout. That particular picture had over one hundred likes and a stream of comments.

Penny the coffee dog.

Penny the Magnificent!

Please send me three pounds of Brazilian Tailfeather and throw Penny in too.

"Whoa! You are really onto something," Martha said, feeling happy for the first time today. "I'd never have dreamed of posting pictures of Penny."

"I must get back to the shop," Octavius said brightly, glancing at his watch and heading for the front door. "We have Any Last Words free writing time starting in ten minutes."

As Margaret followed Octavius out the door and over to Toad in a Hole, Helen went upstairs to fill orders while PJ busied herself ringing up a writer who was purchasing a "See Rock City" bird house with its ubiquitous red sides, black roof, and bold white lettering. Left on her own, Martha realized her stomach was growling. She went in the back and helped herself to some fresh egg salad on wheat bread, planning to sit at the counter to eat and think. When she pushed back through the kitchen door with her plate in her hand, a woman was already seated at the counter, reading the small printed menu. She had on a pair of multicolor readers, her grey hair pulled into a single braid that trailed halfway down her back, and wore overalls, work boots and a long-sleeved t-shirt. Martha didn't recognize her as one of the writers.

When Martha sat a few stools down, the woman eyed her sandwich and asked, "What's good here?"

"Oh, just about everything," Martha replied, thinking she perhaps should have taken her sandwich upstairs. "Can I get you something?"

"Really, I just want a cup of coffee and"—here, she leaned back to get a better view of the dessert case—"a piece of whatever kind of cheesecake that is."

Martha got up and came around to the back of the counter. She poured the woman a cup of Rufous Blend (*always good with dessert*) and cut a slice of turtle cheesecake, then placed both in front of her.

"Mmmm. Thanks. Sorry to interrupt your lunch," the woman said, gesturing at Martha's sandwich.

"Oh, no problem," Martha said, sitting back down and biting into her egg salad.

"I guess you work here?"

Yep, definitely should have taken the sandwich upstairs, Martha thought, resigning herself to a conversation.

"I actually own the shop," she replied in a friendly tone. "It used to belong to my aunt, but she passed away last year and left it to me."

"Oh, so you live in the area?" the woman asked, her tone equally friendly. Martha nodded, her mouth full. "Were you here the other day when Carla Innsbruck was killed?"

Martha nearly choked on her wheat bread, and popped around the counter to reach for a cold soda. Taking a few sips, she sputtered, "Yes, I was. Do you mind telling me why you're asking?"

"Well, I knew Carla. Knew her well, as a matter of fact." She reached forward and patted a manila envelope that Martha hadn't noticed.

"Do you mind if I ask how you knew her? I only ask because I'm... helping the police with their inquiries," Martha said. *Those fibs just flow like water.*

"Hmmm..." The woman sat quietly as if thinking. After about ten seconds, she said, "Well, she was actually my cellmate from 2012 to 2017. She got released in 2017. I didn't get out till 2020, but Carla stayed in touch from her day of release. She even helped me get a job when I got out. I drive a recycling truck. Nothing to brag about, but it's steady income."

"You're kidding! Can you tell me more about Carla? What she was like?" Martha abandoned the remnants of her sandwich and scooted over so that she was right next to the woman. "And by the way, my name's Martha." She held out her hand.

Shaking Martha's hand with a firm grip, the other woman smiled and said, "I'm Debra, but most folks just call me Dee. Nice to meet you. And what can I tell you about Carla? Well, I can tell you I got the luck of the draw when I was put in with her. I'd been to prison before, I'm not proud to tell you, but I won't ever be back in one, and that's mainly thanks to Carla." Her eyes began to water, and she dabbed at them with her napkin. "I'm sorry. It's just... Who in the world would want to kill her?"

"I'm trying to figure that out too, Dee. You see, my friend Mary Jane—she and her sister run the antique store right next door—has been arrested for Carla's murder, but we all know she didn't do it. So I'm trying to uncover everything I can in order to find the real killer. Is there anything else you can tell me about Carla? From what I know so far, she could be pretty strong-willed, with her own way of doing things."

"Oh, that's putting it lightly," Dee laughed through her tears. "Carla drove everyone nuts. The guards, some of the other inmates, and sometimes me. She was so headstrong when she really believed in something. She was bound and determined to get the library in the prison to carry more current books, and she never stopped hounding the board and the warden about it.

"She wrote every literacy organization she could find until book donations started coming in so fast and furious, the warden and board *had* to let her have her way. After that, it was a fresh coat of paint for the library so the warden could send photos to the literacy organizations to show her gratitude. Oh, that really burned her up. Did you know it was Carla who got our prison recycling and composting programs started? That was all her, though the warden never minded the press she got when we became the first prison to receive a Green Award from the state."

"Did you hear about the remarks Carla made at our keynote last week?" Martha asked.

"Read about it in the paper. Makes zero sense to me. As I said, I stayed in touch with Carla. Phone calls here and there, for the most part, but she was still the same old Carla. None of this *Let the Earth Go* crap. I have no idea what that was about."

"Me neither. And from what I've gathered so far, it's not really who Carla was. There has to be some reason she made those bizarre remarks right before she was killed, and if I can figure that out, I might solve this whole puzzle and get Mary Jane out of jail."

Dee looked at her with a serious expression before speaking. "Listen. You're saying your friend is innocent. You also sound like you're not buying the notion that Carla was somehow off her rocker at the keynote. Are you *really* trying to figure out who killed her?"

"Absolutely," Martha said without a pause.

"Then I've got something for you." Dee slid the manila envelope over to Martha. "Carla mailed this to me several days ago and called to tell me that if anything happened to her to give it to someone. It seemed totally bizarre at the time, but she said she thought she was being followed. Let's just say I don't exactly care for the police, so you seem like a better person to trust with whatever's in this envelope."

Carla was more right than she knew, Martha thought. *She was being followed, by a man who'd gotten into something way over his head*. She opened the envelope to find a stapled sheaf of papers, what looked to be a land deed made out to Mockingbird LLC, and a timeline of some kind. The documents contained too much legalese for her to make heads or tails of them.

"Do you know what this is?" she asked Dee.

"Nope. I make it a point to mind my own beeswax. I'm just the messenger," Dee said, holding her hands up with palms out. By this time, PJ had moved closer and was now preparing the large coffee machine for a fresh brew while simultaneously peering over Martha's shoulder.

"Honey, we've got someone right across the way who could probably tell you what all that says," she said.

Martha slapped her forehead. "Duh! Dee, wait just a minute." She pushed a button on her phone, waited a few seconds, then said into it, "Hey, it's Martha here. If you don't have a client at the moment, do you mind coming over to the shop? It's kind of a rush." She listened for a few more seconds, and then replied, "Thanks. See you soon."

No more than a minute elapsed before Tara Jackson pushed through the front door. "Whatcha got?" she asked.

"Here," Martha said, thrusting the collection of papers into the former attorney's hand. "What is all this?"

Martha, PJ and Dee waited while Tara pulled her hot pink readers down onto her face, then flipped through the papers, occasionally turning back to an earlier page to re-read.

After several minutes, she pushed her glasses back onto her head and said, "Well, what you've got here looks to be your garden-variety bait-and-switch."

Dee, Martha and PJ just stared at her. "Huh?" Martha said on their collective behalf.

"Well, the deed is for a piece of land just outside the state park. This document outlines the boundaries and the GPS coordinates, the selling price, et cetera. The page attached to it shows that the company, a shell called Mockingbird LLC, is appealing to rezone the property from private to commercial. But it's the business plan that's listed as an addendum that really holds the key. If you know how to read the fine print—and I'm guessing a high-priced attorney drafted this thing, 'cause the county commissioners would never be able to translate it—you can see that the real plan here is to build a nature center first, but eventually, over the next five years, buy even more surrounding land and turn the whole area into subdivisions and a strip mall."

"Holy sh—" PJ began.

Tara looked up, her eyes wide with shock. "This is huge," she cut in, holding out the papers. "Where did you get these?"

"That makes sense of the survey sticks I saw," Martha said without answering Tara's question. "They covered a much larger area than any nature center would. They went for acres and acres."

"It might even account for the truck that ran you off the road," PJ added angrily. "Someone didn't want anyone nosing around out there."

"Which obviously, according to Sherry, Carla had been doing," Martha said, trying to pull all of the bizarre threads together. "Did she get killed for looking around out there and finding these documents? But why did she say she supported it in the keynote? That makes zero sense."

Ethel Jean's voice interrupted Martha's reach back over to her sandwich. "Oh, isn't this cozy. You four, sitting here with your nice little sandwiches and drinks, while my sister rots in jail." The small woman had come over to the counter, arms across her chest.

Martha said, "Let me introduce you, Dee. Ethel Jean, this is—"

"I don't care who this is. What I care about is you getting off your backside and figuring out who killed that *Kill the Earth* woman so my sister is let out of jail."

Martha pressed her lips together, and then spoke quietly to Ethel Jean. "Actually, I think Dee here may have helped me figure that out. I may know who had a hand in Carla's murder."

"THEN GO TELL YOUR DAMN BOYFRIEND, WOMAN! WHAT ARE YOU WAITING FOR?"

The whole shop fell silent. Laptop keys stopped tapping, shoppers stopped chatting, coffee drinkers paused their slurping. Ethel Jean turned on her heel and went back through the hallway to Silent Sisters.

"I'm sorry," Martha said to Dee. "It's a really hard time for Ethel Jean with her sister Mary Jane being held for Carla's murder. I'd love to talk to you more, but I've got something I need to do. Will you tell PJ here how to reach you?"

"Actually, I was planning to stick around this afternoon, if that's OK? I saw a bookshop across the way I thought I'd check out, so I'll be here for a bit if you need me."

"Sure, sure," Martha said distractedly. "PJ, did Octavius say it's time for free writing at Toad in a Hole?"

"Sure is," PJ answered. "In fact, we've had several of the writers stop in for coffees to go on their way over. I'd say that a good number of them are there right now."

"Perfect. Be back in a bit. Dee, c'mon. I'll show you to that bookshop."

New Canaan, Tennessee, United States, October 15, 1892

MR. HICKS AND THE MEN and boys of the remaining New Canaan families gathered in the library. I would normally have said "gathered after church," but Pastor Taylor departed yesterday. What happens to a village that has no religious center, no man of faith to whom we can turn for solace? How do we remain in communion with that One who is greater than any one of us?

Mr. Hicks shared the news about the rail spur's cancellation with those few who had not yet heard, and there were tears, even from men who thought nothing of plowing a field twelve hours a day, sleeping a few hours, and getting up to clear trees for most of the next day. Mr. Hicks then gave us the news that I never wanted to hear, yet had dreaded would come. He, as well as his wife and children, are leaving New Canaan. It is true that his youngest son endured a terrible bout with typhoid, to the point where we thought we would lose him, but the scrapper fought with all his might and survived. He is still weak, we all know that, but Mr. Hicks can no longer deny his wife her wish to return to England.

"Men, the time has come for us to think of our families first, not of our spirited hopes and dreams." I shall never, as long as I live, forget those words. He told us he and his family were due to leave New Canaan in three days' time, but that he would leave the key to the mercantile, library and church with any who decided to stay and lead the community. No man stood to accept the responsibility. The gathering broke up, all of the faces present reflecting some mix of fear, shock, and utter desperation.

As he left, Mr. Hicks placed his hand on my shoulder and said, "Charlton, you are a natural leader. I have no doubt you will find the place that deserves your leadership, and there is where you will make your home."

But this must, I think, be the end of our dream. Were we far from rational even to imagine that such a place could exist, where we could be a community of equals, of different languages, creeds and abilities, brought together to create something more than the sum of its parts? Was there more I could have done to keep this day from happening?

As the candle burns down here at the kitchen table tonight and I listen to the wind blowing through our two great trees, I wonder how to tell my family tomorrow that the time has come for us to leave what has become our home.

Chapter Fifteen

M artha and Dee walked straight across the green to Toad in a Hole. They were greeted by a library-like atmosphere that was night and day from Martha's previous visit. The store was full of writers, every single table and chair filled with someone typing on a laptop, others sorting through and organizing papers, some crossing things out with pens on the pads that had been included in their welcome bags. They were taking full advantage of these last few hours of writing time.

Dee wandered off to browse. Martha scanned the room and saw to her relief that the whole Murder Squad was present: Karen, Angie, Nick and Liz. When she met Nick's eye, he quickly looked down at the computer that was sitting on his lap.

Still pretending to be a writer, right down to the last few hours.

Margaret was in the center of the room, helping Karen to un-jam a small printer. Martha walked over to Octavius. He was ring-ing up the purchases of one of the writers.

"Thank you so much, and please don't be a stranger. Come back and see us again," he said, handing over the bag of books. His cheerful voice echoed all over the hushed shop.

"Hello, Martha," he said more quietly.

"Hi, Octavius. Glad to see you are getting some more sales," she said, her voice low. "How much longer does this final writing ses-sion go on?"

"Martha, this will be my best month of sales by far for over six months, and we have the President of the Retailers' Collective to thank." He clapped his hands together. Looking up at the wall clock, he said, "They'll wrap up in about twenty minutes and everyone will have the afternoon to rest up and get ready for our closing ceremony this evening. When they leave, Margaret and I are going to clean up the shop. What a lovely weekend it's turned out to be, after such an inauspicious start."

Martha smiled and nodded, her eyes roaming the room. Liz was typing on a laptop at one of the small desks. Karen was opening the back of the printer with Margaret next to her, unpacking a new ink cartridge. Nick sat in an overstuffed chair and gave a weak smile that Martha didn't return. Angie was at a reading table not far from the register.

What better way to spread a message than to give it to the biggest blabber in the bunch?

"Just go along with me for a minute, OK?" she said quietly, only glancing briefly at Octavius. He looked confused, but nodded, brows knitted together.

When Angie looked up, Martha motioned her over.

"Hey, Martha, how are you?" the young woman asked. "This weekend has turned out well. I'm feeling really optimistic about applying to MFA programs, and everybody's been saying—"

"That's great, Angie, just great. Hey, would you do me a favor, please? You seem to know just about all the writers. Would you mind getting a few people to help Margaret and Octavius move the furniture after the Any Last Words session is over?"

The young woman nodded earnestly and opened her mouth to speak, but Martha held up her hand to silence her and leaned her head in conspiratorially so only Angie could hear her.

"To be honest with you, Angie, I feel like I can trust you to keep a confidence. I was going to help them myself, but I've just received some information that is critical to the police in solving Carla Innsbruck's murder. I'm going to swing by the shop to pick up Penny, and then head to my house to put some final notes together before going to the Riley Creek PD."

She lifted her head back up and gave Angie a knowing look and a slow nod. Angie, looking excited, nodded back like a bobblehead superglued to the back of a bucking bronco.

"Got it, Martha. Mum's the word. You can trust me." Angie made a motion as if to zipper her lip.

"I'm counting on you," Martha replied. Turning, she gave Octavius a meaningful look and said, "Octavius, I'll see you at tonight's closing ceremony." He was still nodding in confusion as she exited the bookshop and headed for Birds 'n' Beans.

With so much adrenalin going around her system, Martha had to force herself not to run across the square. Hollering a brief hello to Helen and PJ, she yelled up the stairs to Penny. With an excuse about needing to get something from her house, she opened the door for Penny and made another quick escape. She knew she didn't have much time before Angie spilled the beans.

Martha made it to the cottage with Penny in record time. She'd nearly jumped out of her skin when a mockingbird had called out an ear-splitting screech from a flowering pink dogwood she was passing.

Silly birds, she thought in irritation. *You may be using your voice to scare away other birds, but you're actually bringing more attention to yourself.* She waved an arm and the bird erupted from the branch, a patch of white flashing as it flew away.

Delores was out in her front yard, using twine to tie the tendrils of her emerging clematis so that they climbed evenly up the post of her mailbox. Martha ran over and, in a breathless rush, said, "Delores, can't talk now. Liz Waterson will be coming by. Will you watch for her? And once she's been inside my cottage about ten minutes, call Teddy Perry to have one of his patrol cars come over? Thanks. Gotta run."

She left Delores standing, mouth open, a spool of twine in one hand and garden shears in the other.

Martha unlocked the door and went straight to the French doors to let Penny out to the backyard. The schnauzer had been in the shop for so long, Martha suspected she'd be out there for hours, catching up on the state of the state and dropping a few notes to friends.

OK, Martha reflected. *All I need to do is keep Liz distracted long enough for Delores to get a police officer here. I can fake friendly chitchat that long, can't I?* Just in case, she slipped her pocketknife out of her pack and into her back pocket.

Martha stood in the middle of the kitchen, biting her nails until she heard a knock at the front door. She spread her legs, did her power pose with two deep breaths, and purposefully strode to the door.

You may have killed Carla because she found out about your sketchy land deal, but it ends here.

Swinging the door open, Martha was surprised to find Karen Todd standing on the porch. Martha stuck her head out the door and looked down the street toward Toad in a Hole.

"Uh, hi, Karen. What are you doing here?" she asked.

"Hey, Martha. I hope you don't think it's weird of me to just show up on your literal front step, but I want to chat with you, if you have a minute."

"Um, sure. Come on in. I can't talk long, though. I'm expecting someone."

Martha glanced over to Delores, giving her a "no" shake of the head. Delores shot back a nod of understanding and returned to her clematis.

Closing the door behind Karen, Martha automatically asked her if she wanted a cup of coffee.

"Sure, if it's not too much trouble."

Martha was a little irritated at Karen interrupting her plan, but didn't want to be rude to one of the workshop participants.

"How about I make you a to-go cup?" she asked, thinking that could move things along more quickly. "And how did you know where I live?"

"Sure, a to-go cup would be fine," Karen replied, looking around the living room and reading the spines on Aunt Lorna's books. "Oh, I'd come out this way on a walk one day, and just happened to see you pull in here. It was pretty obvious it was your house. You're really lucky to live in a nice place like this."

Martha went into the kitchen and set about preparing coffee. She stood over the coffee pot, willing it to brew more quickly.

"You're right," she called through to the living room. "My aunt left it to me."

"Mmmm, that's nice," Karen called back. "My husband died, but he didn't leave me much."

Wait, didn't Karen say she and her husband live in Johnson City? As in, he's still alive? Snapping back to the conversation as the thought whizzed across her mind, Martha listened as Karen carried on.

"We'd already lost our house, car, and most of our savings. That's actually why I went back to work editing."

"What do you edit?" Martha asked, feeling like this conversation was going to a weird place.

"Oh, you'll laugh. I edit technical manuals for an appliance company. Washing machines, washers and dryers, even garbage disposals. I make sure they're readable for the average consumer."

Pouring coffee in a to-go tumbler that read "Peckers" and pictured the seven Tennessee woodpecker species, Martha called to Karen, "That must be interesting work. Cream and sugar?"

"No thanks. Just black. Interesting? It's mind-numbingly dull. Not like this life of yours, or Carla Innsbruck's. In fact, I read she'd been about to make a comeback."

Martha came back to the living room where Karen was standing and handed the tumbler to her.

"Yeah, I know. How would someone like *me* know about a thing like *that*? After all, I'm just a lowly technical editor living in east Tennessee, hoping to become a bigtime writer."

They'd moved to the seating area in front of the fireplace. Karen sat in a chair and put her cup down. Martha sat on the couch, close to the door so she could get to it quickly.

"Yes, well, writing of any kind is good exercise for the mind, they say. I'm so glad you've enjoyed the retreat and I hope you'll keep in touch—"

"But, you know, I've always kept a close eye on Carla Innsbruck. A *very* close eye. And when I read in the book section of the paper that she was poiscd to makc a comcback and was the keynote speaker at your retreat, I just *had* to come." Karen's voice had taken on a menacing tone and her face had become flushed.

Holy crap, Martha just had time to think before Penny began pawing at the French doors. Martha made as if to stand to let her in, but Karen grabbed her arm in a vice grip.

"*You stay right here!*" she hissed, then threw herself at Martha, a pillow clenched in one hand. They fell to the floor, Martha trying to hold Karen's arms and the pillow away from her face. "You just *had* to nose around, didn't you? Well, this time, I'll need to be neater. Not like the other night at the church. I had to pick up some hydrogen peroxide to get that little mess out of my clothes. And why, you ask, wouldn't I just get rid of the clothes? Well, for someone whose husband LOST HIS JOB after Carla Innsbruck destroyed it for him, and then died LEAVING HER NOTHING, getting new clothes at the drop of a hat isn't so feasible."

Martha felt the woman's surprising strength as Karen kept a tight grasp on her wrists. Her mind whirled with Karen's words. Her husband? Carla destroyed him?

She pushed away, managing to separate herself from Karen and regain her footing. They faced off like two sumo wrestlers, the coffee table between them. Karen held the pillow in both hands and shifted her weight from foot to foot.

"Karen, what are you talking about? Who was your husband? Why in the world would you kill Carla?" One part of Martha was focused on Karen as a lethal threat, the other still stuck on Liz. "What about the land deal?" she asked desperately, hoping to throw the other woman off and buy herself time. Her mind raced, trying to figure out how to get away.

"What the hell are you talking about? I don't know anything about any land deal. I only know that my husband Ben was on duty at the federal land office that night, just doing his job, when that woman decided to break in and throw blood everywhere. It wasn't his fault, but he got the blame. It had been a good, steady job and he'd done it well, but, thanks to that WOMAN, he lost it. We were happy, but after Innsbruck's antics, he was never the same. *We* were never the same. But as long as she was in prison paying for what she'd done, it was fine.

"Then Ben died and I was left with nothing. When I saw she'd been released, I watched her. I live ten miles away, so I drove by at least once a week. I loved seeing the weeds grow in her yard, seeing things fall down around her."

"But I thought you lived in Johnson City?" Martha said.

"Please. You think I'd live that far away and take a chance on Innsbruck coming down here after prison and having a *life*? No way. If Ben wasn't going to have one, neither was she."

It clicked for Martha. She thought back to when she'd called Johnson City *Little Chicago*. Karen hadn't gotten the reference, which anyone who'd spent any time in Johnson City would have.

"But how did you not have blood all over you at the church? How did you do it?" Martha said, still very ready to run when the moment presented itself. Penny was now whining and clawing at the French doors.

"Easy. Being married to a former Marine who did a few active duty tours, you learn the tricks," she said. "I hadn't really planned to do it there, but when I saw everyone leave and Innsbruck go to the vestry alone, I saw my chance. I walked in, pretended to reach out to shake her hand, and with the other hand pushed the knife straight in. She crumpled slowly to the floor, me keeping the knife tight into her stomach as she lay back. There was some blood, that's true, but the key was not to remove the knife. The blood, for the most part, stays in the stomach cavity. I simply stopped in the ladies room, turned my shirt and sweater inside out, and washed what little blood there was off of my hands. The blood on my black clothes never even showed. Then I went back to the Fellowship Hall."

Martha realized then that she was in the presence of someone without a conscience, and she had to do something quick. She moved around the coffee table and jumped at Karen. The element of surprise she'd hoped for was no use. Karen flipped the balance of power and was soon sitting on Martha's chest, pinning her arms down.

Martha could feel Karen's weight pushing the breath out of her diaphragm. Karen reached back, opened the tumbler, and poured the scalding coffee into Martha's face. As Martha took a sputtering breath in, she felt the velvet pillow come down on her face. There was no way to breathe and Martha was sure her heart was about to come bursting out of her chest. She saw stars popping in the blackness. Her last thought was that she'd never even gotten to try the new bird-friendly coffee Helen had ordered.

Suddenly, light returned and Martha pulled in a desperate coughing breath. Dogs were barking hysterically. The weight on her chest lifted. She blinked against the sting of coffee in her eyes. Delores was standing over her, garden-gloved hands poised in the air. Looking to her right, Martha saw Karen Todd knocked out cold, shards of a terracotta pot scattered around her head.

"Shoot. That was one of my favorite pots," Delores said sadly.

New Canaan, Tennessee, United States, October 16, 1892

WHEN I AWOKE TODAY, it was with resolve to tell Mother and Susannah that we have to leave New Canaan. I rose from bed, feeling the fall chill in the air, and stoked the night's coals back into life with a few lengths of wood.

Mother rose and began assembling tea things. I could not meet her eye, ashamed at having to tell her it was time to return to England and take up my role of second son once and for all. My dream, it seemed, had all been folly.

As I was slipping on my boots, a knock came at the door. Mother and I exchanged glances; no good news had come unbidden to our door these last two months, but I could not think what more bad news could fall upon our household.

I opened the door to find five of the men from last night's gathering. They were the youngest of the bunch, each standing hat in hand. Two were Italian immigrants named Antonio and Giorgio who had come from Boston with their young wives. One, a Black man named Frank, had come from western Tennessee. Tom, a coal miner from Wales, and John, a second son like me from the Canterbury area, completed the group.

I invited them in and asked Mother to excuse us for a few minutes. She went to help Susannah with her dressing. I can't restate the whole conversation here, but suffice to say I was much taken aback.

It was Tom who, in his strong Welsh accent, said, "We'll be plain with you, Riley. We have no plan to leave New Canaan. Most of us have nowhere to leave to, and this is the best home we've ever known.

For those few of us with children, it's their birthplace. We're hoping now, with the typhoid spent, that we can try one more time to make a go of it."

My initial reaction was to reject their words. After all, no train spur was coming to New Canaan and Mr. Hicks was leaving. How could we possibly survive?

Tom and the others seemed to anticipate my objections. "Who cares about the train?" they said. They asked me to think of New Canaan as self-sustaining, a small community of farmers who lived communally, willing to work collaboratively to raise animals and children, never striving to grow large.

I wondered how they thought this was possible, after the terrible winter and subsequent summer with barely any rain. But these five. If any five could make it, these were the men. They each had work-roughened hands and strong backs, and I could say the same of their wives, for those that had them.

The other four gave Tom rough pushes of his shoulder, encouraging him to keep going. He put a hand in his pocket and it emerged with a fistful of keys.

"Here," he said, pushing them into my hand. "We got these from Mr. Hicks." Then, Tom told me the men wanted me to lead the new version of New Canaan, that they trusted me and knew they had a chance if I were to stay and join them. The next moments were a blur as all five voices climbed over one another, trying to convince me. Maybe, they said, we could even rename the village. Canaan means the Promised Land, and we know now that nothing is promised. It is earned through hard work and sacrifice. Maybe a new name would reflect a new start.

I barely knew my own thoughts about this proposal, but I needed Susannah's blessing for the plan. Would she want to raise a baby in such a sparse community? Would Mother try to convince us to leave before another winter set in? Were the fire at the inn, the hard winters, and the typhoid all signs that this community just wasn't to be?

I rushed the men out and told them I would discuss their proposal, and then come to visit them later.

I waited before the fire, trying to think of the right words to say to Susannah and Mother. My head was a jumble of thoughts. Excited and humbled by the prospect of staying and leading these men, I was also drawn to the idea of returning to England and never seeing the back of a plow horse again.

I rose as soon as Susannah and Mother entered, opening my mouth to speak. Susannah walked straight to the table where the jumble of keys still lay, picked through them and came away with one in her hand: the library key.

I looked at her, questioning, and she said, "Your mother and I are going to the library and will be back within the hour. I'm sure you men made a mess of it last night. We'll need to get that tidied up so that it's ready for our grand reopening. I shall be back for breakfast."

She gave me such a smile that I knew our future was clear.

"Oh, and one more thing," she said, turning before closing the door and placing her hand on her belly. "I think this is a boy we'll be bringing into the world. But whether it be boy or girl, what do you think of the name Tommie?"

With a wink and a blown kiss, she closed the door behind them.

Chapter Sixteen

T he afternoon had been a whirlwind. Martha and Delores each had to make statements at the Riley Creek PD, and Martha felt sure that Teddy had been watching through the one-way window as she told her story to Officer Daniels.

Earlier, before the police arrived, Delores had explained that Penny was barking so furiously at Martha's back door, Fritz had started howling. Delores, who had been watching for Liz, decided to go against Martha's instructions and pop across the street to the cottage. A quick look inside, and she saw Karen astride Martha with a pillow over her face.

"I had that pot in my hand," Delores had explained to Martha as they waited at her cottage for the emergency services. "It's the one I usually plant my mint in, or else it creeps all over the garden, you know."

"By the way, is that woman going to be all right?" Martha asked Officer Chip Daniels once she had finished giving her statement.

Chip nodded. "She was already coming around when they got her into the ambulance. She'll have a heck of a headache, but I'd say that's going to be the least of her worries. So tell me"—and here he looked to Martha—"*who* was she again?"

Martha felt somewhat embarrassed. Another motive for Carla Innsbruck's murder had been right under her nose, but she'd been so busy focusing on the land deal and Liz's role in it that she'd nearly become the real murderer's next victim.

"She was married to the security guard at the federal building where Carla broke in years ago and poured pigs' blood everywhere. Evidently, he was fired for not doing his job, and from there things went seriously downhill for him and Karen. She blames Carla for everything that happened to them—his firing, them losing their house, everything. When she heard Carla was going to stage a comeback and the keynote was her first step back into the public eye, she saw red. She registered for the retreat, pretended she wanted to be a writer, then killed Carla the first chance she had."

"But if she was in the Fellowship Hall with all of you the night of the keynote right up until you went to leave, how is it that none of you noticed any blood on her?"

"Simple. She was wearing black. By the time we discovered the body, she was on her way back to her cabin to change clothes."

"So this whole time, we've been looking at Mary Jane and her motives when the real killer, and a way simpler motive, was right here under our noses." Once it was out, Chip realized what he'd said and flushed a red that began at his uniform shirt and extended to the top of his ears. "I mean, of course the Chief has been looking at all angles." He glanced uneasily at the one-way window. "And I was starting to do backgrounds on all of the retreat participants. But those take time, and I'm still learning how to use some of the databases..."

He trailed off. Martha leaned over and touched his arm. She knew from their time together in the winter that he was a hard-working police officer who took his job protecting the citizens of Riley Creek very seriously.

"Chip," she said, "don't worry. We had all interacted with Karen and had absolutely no idea of her background. I don't even know if Karen is her real name. She'd invented a whole persona for this weekend, and none of us could have known who her husband was or that she was here under false pretenses. There's no way anyone could have figured that out in just a day or two."

Chip returned a weak smile. "Thanks," he said, and then added, almost under his breath, "But I don't know that Chief Perry will buy that."

No sooner were the words out of his mouth than the door to the interview room opened and the Chief walked in.

"Give me a moment, will you, Officer Daniels?" Teddy asked.

"Yessir, Chief." Chip took the distance to the door in two long strides and Teddy sat down across from Martha.

"Are you all right?" he asked.

"I'm fine," Martha said, getting ready for Teddy to tell her all the reasons she should have stayed out of the murder investigation. Well, she'd give *him* a piece of *her* mind. It wasn't the 1950s and she wasn't some wilting flower who couldn't manage difficult situations. "Look, Teddy—"

"No, you look, Martha. I'm not here to argue with you or for you to tell me all the ways you are an independent woman who can take care of herself. That's not what this is about. That's not ever been what this is about. It's been about you and me having a chance at something... something real and honest and..." He faded off, as if whatever steam he'd built up had quickly dissipated.

"Teddy, I—"

"Don't, Martha," he said, holding a hand up. "I don't want to hear it. Not this time. I've been in a relationship that was less than honest, and to tell you the truth, I don't have the stomach for another one. I'm glad you are OK, I'm glad your friend will be released from jail. But you and I... we're over. You're not ready for what I have to offer."

With that, he stood up and left the room, leaving the door wide open. Martha sat, her mouth closed and eyes wide.

Jimmy had driven Delores and Martha home from the police station once they'd given their statements and repeated the details more times than Martha could count. The older couple had decided against attending the evening's closing ceremony, but as President of the Retailers' Collective, Martha was determined to be there. She glanced at herself in the mirror and saw that her eyes were terribly bloodshot. The paramedic had told her that the blood vessels had burst from her not being able to draw air for an extended period of time. It sounded like the petechiae would go away, but not for a week or so.

Martha looked down at Penny, who had not left her side since she'd returned from the RCPD.

"Pretty scary looking, huh, gal? Too bad they haven't invented concealer that can be applied to your eyeball." She leaned down and picked the schnauzer up. "And in case I haven't said it yet, thanks. If you hadn't kept up that racket, Delores might not have arrived in time."

She kissed the top of Penny's head and breathed in her doggie smell.

"Bath time for you soon," she said. Those words were enough to get Penny to tear herself away. She wriggled to get down and, the minute her paws hit the floor, ran down the stairs. Martha knew Penny would be straight into her doggie bed, pretending to be utterly exhausted.

And there is the canine version of changing the topic, Martha reflected.

She looked one more time at her reflection, uttered a "*pfft*" at the futility of fixing what she saw, and headed for the shower. The scalding hot water felt to Martha as though it washed away a year's worth of grime. Refreshed, she blew her hair dry and pulled on jeans, her "Fluent in Fowl Language" long-sleeved t-shirt and an anorak fleece since she knew the evening would likely be cool. Going downstairs, she patted Penny goodbye and headed out the door. She'd decided to go to the shop a bit early, then on to the Tarberry House with the others for the closing ceremony.

As she clattered down the porch steps, she spotted Delores coming across the road in her direction. Martha raised a hand in greeting and called to her neighbor.

"Hey, Delores, how ya' feeling? That hot shower sure did feel good."

The two women came together next to Martha's mailbox.

"My dear, I've had all the action I can stand for one day. After I visit with you, I'm going to soak in my tub with a glass of wine for the next hour and even *Fritz* won't be allowed in to bother me."

Together they laughed.

"Martha, there's something I've been thinking about. After you went in your house, I asked Jimmy to drive me to the library so I could get this." She'd been holding something under her arm that Martha hadn't given a second thought to, but now that Delores held it out to her, Martha saw that it was a small leather journal encased in a thin plastic cover.

"What is it?" she asked.

"This, my dear, is the first volume of Charlton Riley's diary from the time he arrived in Riley Creek." She held up a finger, thinking. "Let me restate that. When Riley first arrived here, this village was named New Canaan. It was only through Charlton's leadership and vision that it became a permanent community, and the villagers eventually voted to change its name to Riley Creek as a way of honoring his legacy."

"That's amazing history, Delores. But why are you giving me this?"

"To read, my dear." Delores leaned close. "Now, it *is* a rare book and those are *technically* not to be checked out from the library, but you might say I've got connections and can make this one exception." She shot Martha a wink. "I think you will find his journey... interesting as you continue your own journey here in Riley Creek. I doubt Lorna ever told you, because she didn't put much stock in such things, but you are an actual descendant of Charlton, through Lorna and your mom's side of the family. He was your great-great grandfather."

"No way!" Martha said, eyeing the journal with new interest.

"Way, my dear, way." Delores paused. "It's no surprise that you were chosen as leader of the Retailers' Collective, or that you will keep going when the odds seem stacked against you, just as Lorna always did. It's in your blood."

"Whoa," Martha said, taking all of it in. "I had no idea."

"Most in this village have no idea, and that's how your aunt liked it. Like so much else in her life, that part was private. I only know because I read the diary and figured it out from there. In fact, your cottage? Years ago, Lorna tracked down where Double Oaks, Charlton's home, stood, but all that remained was the fireplace. Your aunt and Jimmy saved every single stone from that, and when she had a fireplace added to the cottage, it was constructed from that very stone."

Martha didn't answer. Too stunned to form the words, she just gazed from the diary in her hand to her dear neighbor, and back again.

"Well, I hear the tub calling me. Have a lovely time tonight. And remember," Delores said, pointing at the diary, "that's our secret."

Martha mimed zipping her lip and, with a hug, the two women parted. Martha watched until she saw Delores close her front door, then she dropped the journal into her anorak pouch and headed toward the square. She needed to get her head clear to deliver a few remarks at the ceremony in a couple of hours, but she struggled to keep her focus on the short walk.

Martha had hoped that Mary Jane would be able to join them for the evening's closing ceremony, but when she'd talked to Albert earlier, he said there was paperwork to be processed and that a judge was not expected to sign her release until the morning.

Not perfect, but I'll take it any day of the week and twice on Sunday, Martha thought.

When she arrived at the shop, PJ, Helen, and Margaret descended on her, each asking a variation on the same set of questions. Was she OK? What had happened? When would Mary Jane get out of jail? Was it true that Karen from the writers' retreat had attacked Martha? She tried to answer as many of their questions as she could as efficiently as she could.

As the crow sounded four o'clock, a familiar voice called from the hallway to Silent Sisters.

"Up yours, crow." Ethel Jean came walking through the hallway, slipping her phone into the thigh pocket of her cargo pants. "That was Albert," she said. "He just went to see Mary Jane to tell her the news. Apparently, she sent a message to pass on to Jessica Fletcher here. She said to say thank you and that she knew you'd find out who killed Carla. Whatever." Ethel Jean looked skyward, as if surviving a near-death experience and solving the murder of a famous public figure were not such a big deal.

As Ethel Jean fell into a seat at the table, PJ let out a low rumble. "Ethel Jean, you have been positively evil to Martha for two days, and I mean evil beyond your normal level of disagreeable. What do you have to say?" The look she gave Ethel Jean did not invite disagreement.

"Thank you," Ethel Jean said in Martha's general direction, crossing her arms over her chest. PJ glowered at her. "Thank you for figuring out who killed that woman and for getting my sister out of jail. Though you sure took your sweet time about it." She looked at PJ with her eyebrows up and chin jutting out, as if to say, "*Happy now?*" PJ eased back in her own chair, her body language suggesting that yes, she was happy now.

Dee, Carla's ex-cellmate, came into the shop, followed by Lew.

"I figured you all would be headed to the closing ceremony, so I can watch the shop," Lew said, taking up a position behind the counter. There were only a few customers in, but Martha was glad he was there so she and the gals could have a few uninterrupted moments.

"Thanks, Lew," she said. "You're a gem."

Dee came over to their table and asked if she could sit with them. Once she was settled, the others quickly caught her up.

Visibly struggling to process all of the dramatic events, Dee said, "But I guess I don't exactly understand. Why did Carla send me the land papers? Why did she say that crazy stuff at the keynote? Was that part of why that lady killed her?"

Martha shook her head. "I still have to put those pieces together," she said, "and I'll start that first thing in the morning. I want to get the closing ceremony behind us, and then I'll turn my attention to that. Someone—particularly Liz—has a lot of explaining to do."

PJ and Helen immediately locked eyes.

"What?" Martha asked. "You two look like the cats that ate the canary."

As PJ opened her mouth to speak, the door of the shop burst open and Joanne, Allison, and a blond boy walked in. Everyone stood and there were hugs, introductions for Dee, and a quick catchup of the last forty-eight hours' events. As they listened, Joanne sat at the table and Allison remained standing. When she had heard the basic details, Allison nodded, then put her hand on the boy's shoulder.

"Everyone, this is Noah. He's going to be staying with me for a while. Noah, this is... well, this is everyone. You'll figure out names as we go."

The boy raised his head slightly, only enough for his eye to roam quickly over the group. Then he faced the floor again.

"Whatever," he said.

Allison looked at the group apologetically, then said, "I'd love to stay and catch up, but I'm going to take Noah home and get settled. Then I need to call Chief Perry to get caught up on everything at the PD." Looking directly at Martha, she said, "Speak soon." Waves exchanged, she slipped back out the door with Noah slouching along behind her.

Joanne blew air out so hard, her bangs moved. "She's going to have her hands full with that one," she said, shaking her head.

Martha looked back and forth from PJ to Helen. "OK, you two. Spill it."

Helen nodded at PJ. "You do it. I was just your trusty sidekick on this one."

PJ looked up at the clock, which now read 4:25. "This will be quick. Once you left, we got to talking about how to figure out what was going on with this land deal and how Carla fit into it. Dee here said that when she was in the federal penitentiary, if you wanted information from someone, you had to have something to give in trade. So... I called Liz Waterson and told her I wanted to know more about the nature center deal and that, in return, I'd give her a huge news story she could write about."

"You *what*?" Martha said in shock. "We don't even—"

At that moment, the back door opened and Liz walked in. PJ waved her over.

"Hope you don't mind me using this door. I parked in your lot back there." Liz walked straight to their table, nodding hello to everyone, and sat, looking eagerly at PJ. "So, what do you want to know?"

"Tell us about the land deal," PJ said. "We know who killed Carla Innsbruck, and Mary Jane is getting out of jail tomorrow. The killer was the wife of the security guard that was on duty when Carla broke in and threw blood all over the building he was guarding. So we know Carla's murder had nothing to do with the land deal, but somehow it—and you—are all tied up in this."

Liz was visibly uncomfortable, trying to take in all of the new information. And she clearly wasn't used to being talked to like that.

"Look, I don't have anything to do with any murder and I don't have to tell you anything. I—"

PJ interjected in a soft voice. "Liz, let me start again. We don't think you had anything to do with the murder. That part is solved. But there's more to all of this, and it's something related to the proposed nature center. Someone paid a guy to follow Carla Innsbruck and take photos of her snooping around that land. Then Martha here looked around out there and nearly got run off the road. She could have been killed. We've had an attorney go over the zoning papers with a fine-toothed comb and she says it's all a cover for a huge commercial development that butts right up against the state park. Now, if you could please tell us what you know, we'd be most appreciative."

Ethel Jean harrumphed.

Liz opened and closed her mouth twice, like a goldfish in search of a bowl of water. A look of dawning realization came over her, then a dark cloud of anger.

"Oh. My. Heavens. I'm taking your word right now that what you're saying is true. If it is, I think I may know who's behind it. My brother-in-law. He's hard up for money, asked me if I'd sign on to this one deal with him, and I did it without many questions. I was even stupid enough to front him ten thousand dollars as seed money for the project. I was busy with the house and thought if I did this one favor, he'd leave me alone. He's always been a leech and involved with the wrong people, even when my husband was living. It sounds like he's trying a get-rich-quick scheme without telling the commissioners the whole story, and he's gotten a fellow scumbag to keep people out of the area. Oh my gosh. How could I have been so stupid? What can I do to make it right?" She looked frantically from face to face around her.

"Tell him to stick his deal where the sun don't shine, for starters," Ethel Jean suggested.

"Consider that done," Liz said. "But how do we stop it from going through? Especially now that Carla Innsbruck all but endorsed it at the keynote."

"Why would she have done that, said all of that crazy stuff about ending the Earth and endorsing the development deal if she didn't really believe in it?" Joanne said. "I know I've missed most of the action and I'm still trying to fit it all together, but that part doesn't make sense to me. Seems like all her crazy squawking would have just made her a spectacle."

At the word "squawk," something in Martha's memory snapped. Didn't the mockingbird do the same thing? Make loud sounds to scare other birds away from their territory, but in so doing, draw attention to themselves and their nests?

Martha realized she had been so focused on Carla's apparent change of heart, she had totally missed the fact that the woman had stated in so many words that the nature center wasn't the driving force behind the land deal; the commercial properties were the real motivator all along. In fact, everyone seemed to have missed that small but crucial detail, even Liz. Nonetheless, Carla had achieved what she set out to do.

Martha spoke to the table of women, processing her thoughts as she went. "Maybe that was *exactly* what she intended. I mean, if she just delivered the keynote we all expected, what would have happened? A fairly nondescript talk, safe remarks about the writing life, et cetera. Instead, she went completely off the rails and said the opposite of what we all expected. As a result, she got more press, and drew way more attention to the nature center project, than she could have done otherwise."

Tentatively, Dee spoke. "You know, you have a point. She kind of did the exact same thing when she was in prison." Seeing a circle of confused faces, she kept going. "See, before Carla was in jail, she was borderline famous. People listened to her and respected her as this outspoken environmentalist. In prison, all that goes away. You have no voice, no influence. The only way she was so successful with the literacy projects was by coming at things from an opposite direction."

"What do you mean, opposite?" Joanne asked gently.

Dee shifted in her seat. "Well, for example, when she wanted the prison library to stock more current books, she knew that just asking wasn't going to result in what she wanted. Who was going to listen to an inmate? So she tried something crazy. When she wrote letters to local charities, she asked them for money to fund a prison museum so that we could highlight the fact that we had some of the oldest books and facilities in the entire state. As you can imagine, this had the opposite effect. No one wants to brag about being the *oldest* in anything. So instead, they started sending brand new books and money for paint. See? She squawked the loudest about something she really didn't want, making the opposite thing happen."

"I'll be damned," said Ethel Jean. "She got attention, all right. Just not the kind she was counting on. Hey, Dee—hand me those papers." Dee handed them over and Ethel Jean reached down the table and gave them to Liz.

"You're a reporter, right?" Ethel Jean asked.

"Well, sort of—"

"You asked what you can do," Ethel Jean went on, ignoring the other woman's hesitation. "What you can do is use those papers to blow this whole thing sky high, and make sure everyone in this village knows what the real plan is for that nature center. People will turn out to the rezoning meeting, all right. And while you're at it, make sure you mention that my sister had nothing to do with that woman's murder. Oh, and be sure to drop Silent Sisters' name and address in there somewhere."

Ethel Jean stood up abruptly and walked through the hallway into the shop she and Mary Jane owned. "I'm going to RCPD to see if those rent-a-cops will let me see my sister now," she called back to those in Birds 'n' Beans. And with that, she disappeared out the door.

Glancing up at the bird clock, Liz slipped the envelope into her satchel and stood. "I'd better head over to the closing ceremony." She patted her bag. "I'm only going to stop in for a minute. Something tells me I've got a long night of writing ahead." Then, she confirmed Martha's suspicions. "It's weird. When Carla said something in her keynote about allowing the land outside the park to be rezoned for commercial use, I knew deep down something was odd about what she was saying. As far as my no-good brother-in-law had assured me, his plan was purely about building a new nature center. But I was so shocked by the famous environmentalist wanting to destroy the Earth, I must have put that to the back of my mind. Anyhow, I'm off now." Out the door she slipped.

Dee stood and gave a smile and nod to the faces around the table. "It's been a real pleasure spending the day in Riley Creek. And I'm glad I found the right people to share Carla's papers with. She was a good friend and I hate that I lost her, but I'm glad you all will make sure people know what she was really about." She teared up a bit, then cleared her throat and pulled her car keys out of the chest pocket of her overalls. "I'm headed back home. PJ has my contact info if there's anything you need from me."

Goodbyes exchanged, she too was gone.

The titmouse on the clock told them it was time to head to the Tarberry House. As the group pushed in chairs and headed for the door, PJ said to Martha, "Honey, do you have one minute to spare before we go? I wanted to show you our online sales for the week. You won't believe it! It'll just take a sec."

"Sure," Martha replied. While the others filed out, PJ retrieved her laptop and hurried back to the table.

"I know this is none of my beeswax, but what are you gonna say to Teddy?" PJ asked as she settled into a chair next to Martha and fired up the machine. "I don't expect he'll take it too well once he figures out you were snooping around Carla's murder this whole time."

"Honestly, PJ, he already knows. I think I've messed up anything he and I might have had, and I've done it good and proper this time." She sighed, feeling a hundred years old, then said, "Maybe this is the right time to just focus on the shop."

PJ nodded. She hit a few keys and said absently, "Well, honey, you know what's best. But I..." She trailed off, not finishing her sentence and staring wide-eyed at the screen.

"What is it?" Martha asked.

"It's... um... I'm not sure, but it..." PJ turned the laptop so it faced Martha. "I'm going to go... make sure we have enough Sheep Dog whiskey for spiked cocoa in case people want to come back here after the ceremony." With that, PJ got up and hurried toward the kitchen.

What in the heck? Martha squinted at the screen to see some small text typed into the private messaging area. It read:

> *My name is Jamie Stevens and I'm trying to contact the owner of Birds 'n' Beans, Martha Sloane. My biological father's name was Lincoln Settler and I think you and I are family—cousins—if your aunt's name was Lorna. Crazy, right? I know. I'm a little hard to reach, but I'll check in*

again later this week to see if you've responded. So... please write back, OK?

Jamie.

Martha sat back and gazed out into the square, her hand reaching into her anorak and feeling the outline of the diary.

Family.

Well, how about that?

Afterword

To help me imagine what Riley Creek might have been like back in the late 1800s when it was fictionally founded, I turned to a wonderful book about Rugby, Tennessee: *Historic Rugby* by Barbara Stagg. I thank the author for putting together such a beautiful book and for documenting Rugby's rich history.

Rugby, also founded by those with larger-than-life dreams of what is possible, sits on east Tennessee's Cumberland Plateau. A few of its historical events made their way loosely into Charlton Riley's origin story, and if I have done my job well, readers will someday make their way to this charming community to spend the day. It takes very little imagination to understand what drew colonists to it in the late 1800s and why a dedicated group of guardians stand watch over it still.

IF YOU HAVE ENJOYED Martha and Penny's adventures so far, be sure to check out the next book in the *Riley Creek Cozy Mystery Series*.

Get your claws on more bird and coffee-related content by signing up for my newsletter at **marylucal.com**. You'll get access to:

- Sneak peeks at upcoming books
- Fun and easy recipes (if I can make them, anyone can!)

- Bird-y trivia
- Exclusive content

About the Author

Mary Lucal is happy to be putting her English and Women's Studies double major to use, creating flawed yet brave female sleuths who get a little help from Mother Nature to solve mysteries.

Mary is the author of the Riley Creek Cozy Mystery Series, including *Hiking Sticks, Hawks, and Homicide* and *Binoculars, Blue Jays, and Bloodshed*.

A university administrator by day, Mary resides in Tennessee and spends her free time birding, hiking, camping, biking, or gardening.

CPSIA information can be obtained
at www.ICGtesting.com
Printed in the USA
JSHW020437010623
42518JS00003B/22